WIF

When illness wrecked her career and her fiancé walked out on her, Juliet was ready to grasp at any straw—and when Damon Masters asked her to marry him, to enable him to take an important job in one of the Gulf states, it suited her to accept. She had no feeling for Damon—or so she thought, until Monique Lamont came back into his life. And by then it was too late.

WIFE FOR A YEAR

BY

ROBERTA LEIGH

MILLS & BOON LIMITED
15–16 BROOK'S MEWS
LONDON W1A 1DR

First published 1980
Australian copyright 1980
Philippine copyright 1980
This edition 1980

© Roberta Leigh 1980

ISBN 0 263 73374 2

Set in Linotype Baskerville 10 on 12 pt.

*Made and printed in Great Britain by
Richard Clay (The Chaucer Press), Ltd., Bungay, Suffolk*

CHAPTER ONE

'THAT'S all for the moment.'

The director's smooth, lilting voice echoed through the auditorium and the four people on-stage relaxed, smiling at each other to relieve the strain of the highly emotional scene they had just enacted.

Watching from the wings, Juliet Stone doubted if she could ever achieve the same magic quality as Magda Carr, the star of the play they were rehearsing. They were due to open in four weeks' time, and tensions were already mounting as members of the cast jostled for good positions on the playbill and programme. Even after five years in the profession, Juliet was still amazed by the egocentricity and petty jealousies of many of her fellow actors and actresses. She had learned her craft the hard way—in small repertory companies—and was so delighted to be a member of this illustrious West End cast that she would gladly have taken bottom billing, or even no billing, in order to have the opportunity of appearing with them.

'Don't forget you're taking me to lunch, Perry,' Lilah Rhodes called out. She was second lead to Magda and was bitterly jealous of every female in the play.

And particularly of me, Juliet admitted to herself, knowing it wasn't her looks that Lilah envied—for the girl was beautiful and talented enough in her own right—but her friendship with Perry Langdon, the director. Perry of the Irish charm and pale-skinned, blue-eyed Irish looks. Perry, who had the ability to make any woman—be she six or sixty—feel more cherished than everyone else. Yes, it was his love for Juliet that Lilah envied; and though Juliet knew she was foolish to be worried by it, she could not overcome her disquiet each time Lilah's slightly protuberant brown eyes rested on her.

'You should have enough confidence in yourself not to be worried by *any* woman,' Perry had admonished her when she had told him how she felt. 'When you belittle yourself, you're belittling *my* judgment. I'm the tops in my profession, darling. Every play I direct is a winner and any actor or actress who works for me is a star. That also applies to the girl I love. If she's going to become my wife, she's the greatest.'

There was no doubt Perry believed what he was saying, and that he expected her to believe it as well, and Juliet knew she could never make him understand the doubts and uncertainties that still beset her; the result of the emotional insecurity that sprang from a difficult childhood. Her parents had been killed in a car crash when she was six, and she had been brought up by elderly grandparents who had not wanted to have their lives disrupted by a youngster. They had given Juliet everything money could buy, but not a great deal of love. They sent her to a select boarding school, saw her only in the holidays when, for the most part, she was left to her own devices, and made no effort to understand the problems of a teenager.

At the age of eighteen she developed a passionate interest in the theatre, and her grandparents paid for her to attend a well-known drama school in London. She was in her second term there when her grandparents died within two weeks of each other. Though she had never felt close to them, she had been saddened by their death, and had felt even more so when she discovered they had used most of their capital to educate her. How much happier she would have been to have stayed at home with them and gone to a day school! But the past could not be changed, nor could the effect that it was going to have on her future, for she discovered that by the time her grandparents' debts had been paid, there was no money left for her to finish her course at drama school.

Leaving at the end of the term, she had managed to get a job as a general dogsbody in a northern repertory company. Gone was the comfortable life of the past, and she had found herself staying in third-rate digs and working all hours of the day and night.

But the harshness of her new life helped her to discover unsuspected depths within herself, and soon these depths were giving stature to the parts she was playing, causing her to be noticed for the special quality with which she imbued her performances.

It was a quality that did not fully emerge until she stepped on to the stage in her first major part. The audience were tough Northerners, but by the end of the first act she had them gripping the edges of their seats, and by the time the final curtain came down she had won every heart in the theatre.

Quick to take advantage of a new and exceptional talent, Jock Worsley, the director, took Juliet under his wing and began to coach her. He was not an easy teacher, but he was a great one; and great enough to know and admit when he could teach her nothing further.

'It's time you started to work with a director who

will help you to extend your range,' he told Juliet on her twenty-first birthday. 'I'm sending you to my friend Perry in London. He's looking for someone to play the ingénue in a new play he's putting on at the Carlton Theatre.'

There was only one Perry in the theatrical world, and Juliet was terrified at the thought of working with him. 'But I'm n-not g-good enough,' she had stammered.

'He'll make you good enough,' Jock had assured her. 'I've kneaded you into a pliable piece of dough, but Perry's the only one who can roll you into shape.'

It was only after she had been with Perry for a month that Juliet realised what Jock meant. Perry only enjoyed working with people whom he could mould. If you resisted him, he discarded you, but if you accepted his advice then there was no one more generous with his knowledge or time.

Juliet fell in love with Perry almost the first moment they met, and Perry said afterwards that he had felt the same. But she had known this was not true. His love had not been aroused until the opening night of the new play, when the audience had given her a standing ovation. Coming on to the stage to take his bow with her, he had caught her hand and looked deep into her eyes.

'You are my creation, Juliet,' he had said. 'There'll be no stopping us now.'

With a swiftness that was typical of him, Perry took over her entire life. He chose her clothes, her hairstyle and her make-up. He told her what books to read and what music to hear. He shaped her on-stage and off, forming her into his idea of the perfect woman. Then, having created her, he had asked her to become his wife.

Juliet could not envisage any greater happiness for herself. She felt as if she had everything: youth, beauty, success and a brilliant man who wanted her to share his life.

'We'll get married at the end of the summer,' he promised, 'and we'll honeymoon in America. I want to show you off to all my friends on Broadway and in Hollywood.'

'Why can't we get married now?' Juliet had pleaded, for it was only May, and autumn had seemed a long way away.

But Perry would not be hurried. 'My marriage to you will be a full-time occupation for the first three months,' he had teased. 'I've made you the perfect star and I'll need time to make you the perfect wife.'

His blue eyes had sparkled with mischief, though the fire burning deep within them had told her he was not joking. If she had loved him less she might have objected more to his desire to shape her into what he wanted, but because she adored him she felt only pleasure at the thought.

Juliet remembered this now as she left the wings and waited to see Perry before he went out to lunch. Three more months until September and she became his wife. She glanced at her hands, wishing she could wear a ring to show that she belonged to him. But Perry was disdainful of engagement rings, saying that all couples had them and he wanted to be different.

'Does that mean I won't have a wedding ring either?' she had asked.

'I'll get you one if you insist on it,' he had said. 'But

my token of love to you will be a diamond heart for you to wear around your neck. I've already ordered it.'

She had been so delighted at his sentiment that she had flung her arms around him and kissed him with abandon, wishing, as she often did, that she was truly his. But in this respect, too, he had surprised her.

'You're going to be my virgin bride, Juliet. I was lucky enough to find one—a rarity in our profession— and I won't do anything to spoil that image.'

'You and your images!' she had laughed. 'Do you know that Magda calls them your obsessions?'

'Magda's a cynic. You shouldn't listen to her.'

Juliet had smiled, knowing that she listened to no one except Perry, and that he knew it.

'Day-dreaming, darling?'

His melodious voice, light and soft as an Irish mist, broke into her thoughts and she spun round to see him beside her. He exuded such dynamism that she was always surprised, when standing close to him, to realise he was only a few inches taller than she was. They could have passed for brother and sister, for they had the same dark, glossy hair and creamy white skin. But where Perry's eyes were blue and marked by fawnlike eyebrows, Juliet's were sherry brown and large as those of a gazelle, with eyebrows delicately arched above them. She had a gazelle-like grace too, with long slender arms and legs, a fragile stem of a neck, and a willowy body redeemed from boyishness by small but well-defined breasts.

'I wish you weren't lunching with Lilah.' Juliet's voice, like her appearance, was delicate yet clear. 'I feel as if you're going over to the enemy camp.'

'You're too imaginative, darling.' Perry raised her hand to his lips. 'Stop worrying about someone as unimportant as Lilah and go to your dressing room for a rest. You look tired.'

'I am a bit,' she confessed. 'Rehearsing for a new play while you're still appearing in an old one is like being back in repertory.'

'It's only for a short season,' he reminded her. 'Three months of hard work, and then we'll be off to the States.'

'And married,' she whispered.

'And married,' he agreed, dropping a kiss on her small straight nose before he went lithely on his way; a dark form in tight-fitting black slacks and matching silk sweater.

Juliet was halfway towards her dressing room when she decided she could not face the prospect of staying there alone for several hours. Besides, though she was tired she was also hungry. Starving, in fact. She pursed her lips and fought with her conscience. Perry liked her to be slim to the point of thinness, and it required constant vigilance to remain underweight. Even if she had been half a stone heavier, she would still have been a slender girl. Suddenly angry at the thought of Perry lunching with Lilah, while she herself was expected to subsist on air pies, she marched towards the stage door. To hell with dieting! She would treat herself to a milkshake and a sticky bun.

Outside in the busy street she lost some of her enthusiasm. If she ate too much today, she would have to be twice as careful tomorrow. Perhaps it wasn't such a good idea after all. She was standing on the kerb, waiting for a bus to pass and wondering if she should return to her dressing room, when her legs started to tremble.

A gleaming maroon car was driving directly behind

the bus, its square bonnet proudly proclaiming it a Rolls-Royce, and she wished it would hurry and go past her, so that she could cross the road to the café and at least get herself a cup of coffee. It was almost abreast of her when her knees buckled beneath her and she pitched forward directly into its path.

Behind her someone shrieked and she tried to stand up to assure them she was unhurt. But the lower part of her body refused to move, and before she could try again, the driver of the car was bending over her and raising her up. He set her on her feet, but as he did so her legs gave way again, and with an exclamation he lifted her into his arms as easily as if she were a rag doll.

He was the tallest man she had seen, and had the physique of a rugger player. Surprisingly, his face did not match his build, for he had lean, fine-cut features, with a long, aquiline nose and a well-shaped, thin mouth. But he exuded strength, for which she was surprisingly thankful, and she relaxed against him with a sigh.

'I'm sorry to be such a nuisance,' she said.

'You could have been killed!' There was no gentleness in his voice, which was deep and firm—only anger. 'If my brakes weren't first class you would have been under the wheels. Didn't you see me coming or did you step out without thinking?'

'I didn't step out,' she protested. 'My legs suddenly gave way.'

'I'm not surprised. You look as if you've just come out of a concentration camp. Fashion!' He almost exploded the word.

'Fashion?' she repeated, puzzled. 'What's that got to do with my legs trembling?'

'It's the reason you're so thin, isn't it? If you get any thinner, you'll disappear.'

Carefully he set her on the pavement, his hands hovering near her as if afraid she might fall again. But her legs were steady and she felt much better.

'I'm sorry I gave you such a fright,' she apologised. 'Please forgive me.'

'Get yourself something to eat,' he said abruptly. 'You'll soon be too thin even to play Camille.'

He strode off without another word and Juliet watched him climb into his Rolls and drive away, before she pushed open the stage door and entered the theatre. The door swung shut behind her, blocking out the sound of the street and obliterating any more thoughts of the man who had rescued her.

'You've had a quick lunch,' the doorkeeper commented as she passed his cubicle.

'I didn't have any at all,' she explained. 'I nearly got run over, so I decided to come back and lie down for a while.'

'Want me to get you a cup of tea and a sandwich?'

'That would be lovely.' She grinned at him. 'And you might as well make it two sandwiches while you're about it.'

She was resting on the lumpy settee when he brought them into her dressing room. He had added a packet of crisps to her order.

'From me to you,' he said lugubriously.

'You're an angel!'

'Make sure you don't become one,' he growled, and gave her a fierce look. 'You're the best thing around this theatre, Miss Stone.'

'A very little stone,' she replied. 'My departure wouldn't even cause a ripple.'

'A girl about to be married shouldn't say a thing like that. What would Mr Langdon think?'

'He'd be as indignant as you are,' she agreed, and bit into her sandwich.

It had a thick filling of cheese and pickle and she thought how angry Perry would be with her for eating it. For a fleeting instant she felt an unexpected rush of self-pity, then she quickly pushed it away. It must be reaction from my near accident, she decided, and gave the doorkeeper a smile as he went out.

I'm not frightened of Perry, she told herself, but she knew she was not being honest. Something about him did make her nervous. It was a pleasurable fear, but a fear nonetheless.

CHAPTER TWO

LOOKING back on it afterwards, Juliet marvelled that she did not have the faintest premonition that something was wrong with her. Even a second attack of paralysis the following day did not alert her, other than to remind her that the tall, irate giant who had rescued her the first time might have a point when he had said she was too thin.

'You aren't too thin,' Perry commented that night as they dined together after the show and she suggested having pasta as her main course.

'Wouldn't you love me if I were plump?' she asked.

'No.' It was unequivocal. 'I love you the way you are.' He tilted his head and the mocking look she loved so much came into his face. 'You're my creation, Juliet, and I'm the only one who's allowed to change you.' He slid across the banquette seat and pressed his thigh against hers. 'In a few months you'll be mine.'

'I wish I were yours now. Why can't we get married before the end of the play?'

'I've already told you why. We're both working so hard we'd have no time together. Be patient a little longer, angel.'

Juliet sighed and let the subject drop. Once Perry made up his mind about something, nothing would change it.

The next two weeks proved Perry right. His revival of an Oscar Wilde play kept her on stage almost half of each evening, as did the new play by a young dramatist which followed a month later. It was an exhausting role and she only had a short respite in the middle of the second act.

One night, after her break, she was waiting in the wings for her cue when her legs crumpled beneath her. She reached out for a chair but could not prevent herself falling, and the noise of it echoed loudly across the stage.

Almost at once Perry was kneeling beside her, his eyes blazing with anger.

'Damn it, can't you be more careful?'

'I couldn't help it,' she said breathlessly. 'I fell.'

'You aren't usually clumsy.'

'It had nothing to do with clumsiness. My legs gave way.'

He was instantly concerned. 'Are you all right now? You're on in a minute.'

Juliet allowed him to help her up. She found she could stand normally and her heart slowed its pace.

'I'm fine, Perry. It was just one of those things.'

'Maybe you *are* a bit too thin,' he said abruptly. 'A couple of pounds more won't make any difference to you.'

'Thanks.'

Her tone was so dry that he gave her a sharp look. But before he could make any comment, she heard her cue and walked back on stage.

Three days later her legs gave way again. This time she was in the middle of her big scene and was moving towards the male lead when she collapsed in front of him.

With commendable presence of mind he picked her up and turned the action into part of the play. But Juliet was so distressed by the experience that it required all her control to continue acting. She was convinced her trembling was not caused by dieting. The fear which she had managed to ignore this past week crystallised into the conviction that there was something seriously the matter with her.

'I'll take you to see Bob Clarendon,' Perry said when she finally came off stage. 'He's my own G.P. and he's first class. I'll ring him and say we'll be along as soon as the curtain comes down.'

'There's no desperate rush,' she protested. 'It can wait until tomorrow.'

But Perry refused to listen and, revelling in his concern, Juliet drove with Perry late that night to Dr Clarendon's home in Chelsea.

Despite it being nearly eleven-thirty, his examination was thorough, and after he had finished, he bluntly told her she should see a neurologist at once.

Her fears intensified, but she forced them back and glanced at Perry. 'You see, darling? Waiting to marry you has made me a bundle of nerves!'

'You aren't suffering from nerves,' Dr Clarendon said. 'The weakness in your legs may be due to some disintegration of the outer sheath that protects the nerves themselves.'

'That's multiple sclerosis,' Perry said at once.

'I don't think this is,' the doctor assured him. 'But the one man who will be able to tell you for certain is Damon Masters. I only hope we can get to see him quickly. The last time I tried, he had a three months' waiting list.'

'I'll get him to see Juliet long before that,' Perry said imperiously. 'I have a few strings I can pull.'

The doctor looked at Juliet. 'Don't look so desolate, Miss Stone. If anyone can help you, Masters can. He's one of the top men in his field.'

He was also, it seemed, one of the few who was immune to Peregrine Langdon's influence. Neither a duke nor a building tycoon could persuade him to see Juliet in under six weeks, and even then it had to be on a Sunday morning.

'He sounds as if he works even harder than you,' Juliet said to Perry.

'Or else he works short hours.' Perry did not like to be thwarted, and showed it. 'I'll ask Robin to ring him again.'

'Don't,' Juliet pleaded. 'It might put his back up. Dr Clarendon sent him my case notes and he wrote back saying he didn't think it was a matter of urgency.'

'It's urgent for *us*,' Perry fumed. 'You can't go on stage in case you collapse, and it isn't easy to get someone to take your place for a short run.'

'Betty's a good understudy.'

'For a few nights only. She has no pulling power at the box office, and if we go on using her the bookings will fall off.'

'What about Lilah?' Juliet said reluctantly. 'She knows my part.'

'I didn't think you'd like me to use her.'

'You won't be using her as a woman,' Juliet whispered, winding her arms around his neck.

'The actress and the woman are indivisible,' Perry said against her lips, and with an unusual display of ardour began to kiss her.

With a sigh of pleasure Juliet pulled him down until he was half lying upon the settee. If only Perry would stay with her tonight! She was afraid of the hours alone, when dark thoughts came to trouble her and she had to get out of bed to make sure she could still use her legs. But she dared not tell Perry. For his sake as well as her own, she had to believe her illness was a temporary condition which would disappear with the right treatment. Yet in her heart she knew she was blinding herself to the truth. There was something seriously wrong with her, and sooner or later she would have to face it.

'You're a witch,' said Perry, pressing his mouth to the shadowy curve between her breasts, before he pushed her away.

'My spell over you doesn't seem to be all that strong,' she pouted.

'Only because my desire for you to be pure is stronger.'

'Do you intend to keep me pure when we're married?'

'It's a virgin bride I want, not a virgin wife.'

Juliet pondered on his words long after he had left. It was strange that a man in the theatrical world should have such an old-fashioned attitude. But then Perry was unique in every way. That was why she had accepted his judgment when he had advised her not to appear on stage until after she had seen Dr Masters.

'It would be too disconcerting for the cast and audience if you collapsed again in the middle of a performance,' he said. 'I know you don't *feel* ill, but it will be much better if you do as I say.'

Of course she had agreed, though giving up her work, even temporarily, increased her fears, and she soon became too afraid to leave her apartment. She spent most of her time reading or listening to music, but sometimes she was too depressed even to do that, and just sat at the window staring into the street and brooding.

One evening Perry admitted he had given her part to Lilah.

'She doesn't have your subtlety as an actress,' he said, 'but she makes up for it with extra vitality. It's amazing how someone else in a part can totally change the character of a play.'

'For the better?' Juliet asked jealously.

'Differently,' he smiled, and stretched out his legs in front of him with a contented sigh.

He relaxed infrequently, but when he did he was like a pampered cat: indolent and ready to be waited on. Juliet liked Perry best at these times, for it gave her an opportunity to fuss around him.

She went into the kitchen to fetch the coffee. Perry had come to see her straight from the theatre, and she knew he had refused many invitations to do so. He was gregarious and loved being the centre of attention, yet he always wanted to have Juliet beside him. He would frequently hold her hand and draw it to his lips, almost as if he wished to proclaim his ownership of her; to bring everyone's attention to her beauty and youth and then show that she was his.

The percolator bubbled and Juliet set it on the tray beside the cups. She took a small jug of cream from the refrigerator and put it next to the petits fours which she had bought that morning: little delicacies of ground almonds and cinnamon, of marron and puff pastry.

Picking up the tray, she went to the door. Without warning her legs gave way and she fell to the floor. The percolator and cups went flying and hot liquid splashed over her foot. For an instant shock held her rigid, then pain from the scalding coffee and anger at her stupidity made her burst into tears.

The noise brought Perry in with a rush. Muttering beneath his breath, he lifted her up and set her on a chair, then bent to look at her ankle.

'Pour some milk in a bowl,' she said shakily, 'and I'll put my foot in it.'

'In milk?'

'It's the best home-made remedy for a scald.'

He did as she told him, and though she was still trembling from shock, she reached over for the kitchen scissors and cut off the bottom of her stocking.

'Tights have so many disadvantages,' she laughed, trying to ease the tension.

He grunted and placed a small bowl of milk on the ground in front of her. She put her foot into it, biting hard on her lip to stop herself crying out. But after the initial shock, the pain subsided and she gave a sigh of relief.

'I'll phone Bob Clarendon,' Perry said.

'There's no need. It isn't a bad scald.'

'Why didn't you ask me to carry in the coffee? You know you shouldn't do anything like that.'

He hadn't thought of it when she had gone in to prepare a snack, but she knew better than to say so. She was surprised by her inward criticism of him, for normally she enjoyed waiting on him. But things were no longer normal, a little voice told her, and might never be normal again. With an effort she made herself smile.

'Don't look so worried, Perry. Nothing terrible happened to me.'

'Only by the grace of God.'

His accent was more Irish than usual and showed her how disturbed he was. It made her feel better, and the smile she gave him was more genuine.

'I'm sorry for messing things up, Perry. For not being in the play and—and getting ill like this.'

'What a foolish angel you are! You didn't do it on purpose. A few months from now and this will all seem like a bad dream.'

'If only I could believe that!' she sighed.

'You've got to believe it. I'll call Dr Masters myself in the morning and see if I can hurry him up.'

But once again Perry had no success, and Juliet swallowed her impatience and reminded herself that three more weeks would soon pass.

But how slow they were to do so. The scald on her leg healed, but the skin was still reddened and was a constant reminder of her illness. Occasionally she went for a walk, but she was always scared of falling. It increased her despondency and, two weeks before her appointment was due, she telephoned Dr Masters' consulting-rooms to see if a personal appeal could prevail on him to see her earlier.

'There's absolutely no point in your talking to Dr Masters,' his secretary told her. 'We already have a note by your name to say you can come at short notice if there's a cancellation. But Dr Masters is only here four afternoons a week, and——'

'Is there a chance of my seeing him at the hospital?'

'You would have to wait even longer.'

'If I could speak to him ...'

'It wouldn't be any use, Miss Stone. Dr Masters is leaving for Doria in the morning, and will be away for a week.'

Disheartened, Juliet replaced the telephone. Unable to concentrate on a book or television, she went to the bookshelf and idly picked out an atlas. Where on earth was Doria? The name was familiar, but she couldn't place it. A glance at the index told her it was a tiny state on the Arabian Gulf. Dr Masters was probably flying out to see some oil rich sheik, and she wondered cynically whether his money had smoothed the way to an early appointment.

Replacing the atlas, she went into her bedroom. Her skin, usually creamy as a tea rose, had the pallor of a magnolia, and she pinched her cheeks to bring some colour into them. But it faded quickly and she turned from the mirror and on an impulse decided to go to the theatre to see Perry. She would hold on to the banisters as she went downstairs and take a taxi instead of a bus.

Not giving herself time to change her mind, she put on a toffee silk shirtwaister. It gave a little warmth to her skin and deepened the sherry gold of her eyes. She brushed her hair away from her face and then, because this accentuated the high cheek bones and revealed the hollows beneath them, she pulled her hair forward again, letting the ends lie like glossy plumage on her cheeks.

Perry did not like her to wear much make-up, and she was frugal with her lipstick and mascara. Even so, the thinness of her face made her lashes look long enough to be false, and she almost wiped off the mascara. She tightened her belt another notch. At least Perry would be pleased that she was so thin.

Unexpectedly she remembered the tall giant of a man who had rescued her when she had collapsed in the street. He had jumped to the conclusion that she had fainted from hunger and would be surprised to know it had nothing to do with dieting but was caused by some unknown disease which was threatening to turn her entire life upside down. The horror of it all engulfed her again, and she pushed back the dressing table stool and ran out.

By the time she reached the theatre she was feeling more cheerful, and had almost convinced herself there was nothing wrong with her that a prolonged rest could not cure. She was relieved that Fred was not in his cubbyhole by the stage door, for she was in no mood to face his sympathy, and she walked down the corridor, slowing her pace as she approached the dressing room that had been hers. Was Lilah occupying it, or had she been given another one?

She reached the door, hesitated and then knocked. There was no reply and she went in. A quick glance told her Lilah was indeed in possession: make-up was strewn over the dressing table. Shoes lay haphazardly on the floor and several dressing gowns in vivid colours hung in the curtained alcove.

Closing the door on the sight, she went in search of Perry. It was four o'clock and the matinée performance was half-way through. That meant he was either watching it from the wings or was in his office dealing with the innumerable day-to-day problems that beset a director/manager.

As she was so near to the stage she continued walking towards it. There were a few people in the wings and some scene shifters were busy moving some flats. There was no sign of Perry and she pushed open the fire door that led into the plushier part of the theatre. Here were the offices of the executives. Perry's room was at the end and she went towards it, excited at the prospect of seeing him.

She reached his office. There was no reply to her knock and she went in. His secretary was not at her desk and the cover on the typewriter showed she had left for the day. The door leading to Perry's room was partly open and Juliet heard his voice. Not wishing to disturb him if he was interviewing someone, she perched on the edge of the desk and waited.

'If you don't tell me I've got the part permanently, I'll definitely accept Marius's offer.'

It was Lilah speaking, her voice angry and loud.

'I can't give you Juliet's part,' Perry said. 'Not until I know whether or not she's coming back.'

'That might take months, and I can't afford to wait. I have to know something definite now. If you don't think I'm good enough....'

'Of course you're good enough.' There was admiration in Perry's voice. 'You have a vitality that reaches out to the audience. If you took over the role permanently I'd put a lot more action into it for you. In your scene with John I'd——'

'I know what to do,' Lilah cut in eagerly. 'That's why I hate all this waiting.'

'Juliet's seeing Dr Masters in two weeks.'

'I won't wait that long!'

'You must. After Juliet, you're the best actress I have.'

'I'm better than she is,' Lilah retorted.

'Not yet, my angel.' There was laughter in Perry's voice, and something more as well. 'But you could be if you were prepared to listen to me.'

'I always listen to you.'

'No, you don't. You're too independent.'

'Only because I've never had anyone who wanted me to be otherwise. No director gives an actress the coaching that you do.'

'That's why I'm the best,' he said with satisfaction.

'And that's why I want to work for you.' Lilah's

voice was husky. 'Do for me what you did for Juliet. I'll be better than she was. I'm stronger and I've got more energy. I won't get sick and let you down.'

There was a rustle of taffeta and Perry gave a muffled groan.

'You're a witch,' he said thickly, and then there was silence.

Juliet slid down from the desk. Her heart wasn't racing and she had no sensation of hurt. All she felt was a deep sense of the inevitable, as if she had always known that Perry and Lilah would come together.

Quietly she tiptoed to the outer door and closed it behind her. She did not blame Perry for what had happened. The characteristics she loved in him made him receptive to the Lilahs of this world. He worshipped success and all it signified. Above all he saw himself as a creator.

Lilah wanted Perry because she craved success. She did not want him as a man, and once she had learned all she could from him, she would look for the next man to help her. Perry did not know this, but Juliet was sure of it. He had a singlemindedness which made him impervious to what other people were thinking. This was part of his strength, but it was also his weakness. For him, Lilah was someone he could mould; someone who would replace Juliet, his last creation, who had cracked.

'But not permanently,' Juliet muttered, and headed for the street. As soon as she was well, Perry would have no more time for Lilah. Damn Dr Masters for keeping her waiting like this! Suddenly she could not face another two weeks of limbo. She had to know the worst or the best—right now. Only when she did would she be able to plan for the future.

A taxi stopped in front of her to deposit a fare, and without pausing to think she climbed in and gave Dr Masters' address in Harley Street. It was a good thing she had looked up his telephone number that morning and remembered his address; it was as if she had had a premonition she would need it.

The cab moved forward and she settled back, hands clasped together in an unconscious attitude of prayer.

CHAPTER THREE

The fine terylene curtains at the tall windows let in the late afternoon sunlight and gave the room a mellow radiance which softened the severe lines of the large desk and the black leather wing chair behind it. It was a massive chair, well suited to the man who occupied it.

At this moment he was bending over some papers, a gold pen in his hand. He wrote busily for a short while, then paused and bit on his lower lip with strong white teeth before starting to write again. He filled another page with small black writing, then slipped the pen into his jacket. There was a rustle of paper in his breast pocket and he put in his finger and pulled it out. It was the stub of a ticket for the Carlton Theatre. He looked at it thoughtfully, then screwed it into a ball and dropped it into the waste paper basket.

Lord knew why he had given in to a sudden impulse and gone there. He was cautious not only by nature but by years of rigorous training in a profession that called for careful judgment. Yet four weeks ago he had returned to his consulting rooms and asked his secretary to get him a ticket for the play at the Carlton.

Miss Benson had been surprised. Normally he only visited the theatre when he was entertaining dignitaries from out of town or abroad. Left to his own devices, he stayed at home, switched the telephone through to his Registrar and then relaxed with the latest medical journal.

But something had impelled him to see the girl again; to find out if she would intrigue him as much on second sight as she had at first. It was more than her physical beauty which had appealed; he was too used to women—of all shapes and sizes—to be susceptible to this alone. But she had an elusive quality about her that had attracted him, and which he had continued to feel long after he had picked her up from the road and deposited her at the theatre door.

She had been as light as a bird in his arms and had the same look of helplessness, until one stared into her huge golden-brown eyes and saw the indignation there, as if she were furious with herself for falling in front of his car.

Seeing her on stage at the theatre later that evening, he had again been struck by her fey quality; only this time it had been allied to a dramatic performance of such intensity that he had been astonished. Likening her to a bird had been apt, for in the same way that he was frequently surprised by the vibrantly sweet notes emanating from minute throats, so had he been at witnessing the girl's brilliantly alive exposition of a character which, until now, he had always found tedious to watch.

During the interval her name had been on many lips, bringing him up to date with her recent success in a world that was as alien to him as he was sure his would be to her.

He had returned home refusing to think beyond his impetuous action, and hoping that a good night's sleep would bring back his normal logic. But it had done nothing of the sort, and he had been irritated with himself. He was no callow youth to be bowled over by a will-o'-the-wisp girl with a breathless voice. He was a man of stature, held in high esteem by men of esteem. His life was full and he had no need of a woman, other than the occasional discreet affair to satisfy a physical need.

Yet a week later he had returned to the theatre, determined to send a note backstage, inviting Miss Stornaway to have supper with him.

Annoyance had vied with relief when he discovered that another actress had taken over her part: a voluptuous creature with none of Julia Stornaway's expressive subtlety. It was funny he should still remember her name when he now found it difficult to recollect her face. A month from now and both would be forgotten. And a good thing too. Had she been appearing on stage that night, he might have made a complete ass of himself.

He pressed the buzzer on his desk and leaned back in his chair. Against the black leather, his dark hair almost disappeared, only the powdering of silver at his temples remaining visible. His suit was black too, discreet in colour and faultlessly cut, as befitted a man in his position.

Damn my position, he thought tiredly. One day I'll pack it all in and take a schooner round the world. The notion vanished as his secretary came into the room in answer to his call.

'We should remember this day, Miss Benson.' His voice was deep and quiet and not given to much expression; a habit he had formed in his student days. 'I can't remember the last time I finished so early.'

'It's only because your last patient cancelled,' Miss Benson said. 'I hope it means you'll go upstairs to rest before you go off to your dinner.'

'I might even cancel my dinner. I have a long flight

ahead of me. Actually I thought of dropping in to the hospital instead. There's a patient I want to see.'

'One day you'll just drop,' Miss Benson said with an honesty that came from seven years in his service.

'I'll have a long rest on the flight tomorrow,' he replied, and gave her the charming smile which had kept her his devoted slave despite long hours and hard work.

Somewhere in the distance a doorbell rang and Damon Masters glanced automatically at his wrist-watch. 'If that's the patient who cancelled....'

'He wouldn't come now.'

The bell rang again and Miss Benson took a step backwards. 'Miss Smith has already left for the evening, Doctor. I'd better go and answer it.'

As his secretary went out, Damon Masters relaxed again. The door was closed, the walls were thick and no sounds came to disturb him. It wasn't a bad idea to close his eyes for a moment and rest. His lids fell, then rose again. If he dozed off, he would be too tired to go out. That was always the danger if one lost a bit of steam during the day. The only thing was to push on until it was time for bed.

Stifling a yawn, he rose and stretched his arms above his head. He would leave the car in the garage and walk to the hospital; the exercise would do him good. With a stride that was curiously light for such a big man, he went to the door.

The hall was empty. Whoever had rung the bell must have been sent away. He was half-way across the marble floored lobby when he heard voices in the waiting room, the door of which was partially open. One of the voices was raised, high with anger and desperation.

'Why can't I see him if he's here? There's no one else waiting. It isn't all that late.'

'It's six o'clock.' It was Miss Benson, trying to calm down the angry visitor. 'Dr Masters is on his way to hospital to see a patient.'

'I'm a patient too—at least I've been waiting three weeks to become one. I've got to see him! I can't go on any longer.'

'It's only another week, Miss Stone.'

'I don't suppose a week means anything to you.' The voice wobbled, as though tears were near, then lapsed into silence.

Frowning slightly, Damon Masters went to the cubbyhole behind the receptionist's desk and collected the key to his Rolls. It would be quicker if he drove to the hospital. With luck he might manage a walk later tonight. As he turned round, the door of the waiting room opened. Quickly he stepped into the alcove beside the lift. It would be too bad if he was seen now, after Miss Benson had done her best to protect him.

His secretary came out, followed closely by a slight figure in beige. He pressed further against the wall and remained motionless as the girl moved to the door. In the light coming in from the transom high above her head, he saw her clearly for the first time, and gave an exclamation of astonishment. Hearing it, the girl swung round to face him.

'You!' she exclaimed in surprise, and took a step forward. 'What are *you* doing here?'

'I rather think that's my question.'

'I've come to see Dr Masters.' She glanced irritably at the woman behind her. 'But it's impossible. Everything here goes by the book.'

Not waiting for his reply, she turned to the door again, moving with the grace he remembered seeing on the stage. She was a pace away from the front step when she crumpled, and though he was quick, he was not quick enough to catch her. She lay on the ground, legs bent beneath her, her huge eyes, like golden-brown lamps, sparkling with tears.

'You see,' she said vexedly. 'It has nothing to do with my dieting.'

'I do see,' he replied in an expressionless voice, and bending forward, lifted her effortlessly into his arms. 'And now I think I really had better see you.'

'You?' she repeated the first word she had spoken to him.

'Who better?' A slight smile touched his grave features. 'You did want to see me, you know. I'm Damon Masters.'

Juliet relaxed against the pillows and felt the firm hospital bed beneath her body. It was hard to believe she was in a private ward in an eminent teaching hospital, under the personal care of Dr Damon Masters.

Things had happened so quickly after she had seen him, that she was still in a state of shock. She remembered her astonishment at discovering that the man who had rescued her in the street was the world-famous neurologist whom Dr Clarendon had recommended. His examination of her had been exhaustingly thorough, and not until it was over had he told her he wanted her to go into hospital for tests.

'Don't you know what's wrong with me?' she had asked.

'I would prefer not to commit myself until I've seen the results of your tests.'

His deep voice had been gentle but firm, and she had known he was not a man one could force into giving an answer.

'When do you want me to go?'

'Today.'

The quickness of it frightened her and he saw it.

'You won't die if you don't,' he said easily. 'But I'm flying to the Middle East tomorrow and I wanted to have you in hospital, with various tests organised, before I left.'

'How long will you be away?' she asked.

'A week. But my absence won't make any difference to you. Some of the tests I want will take several days to do, so by the time I return I should have everything in front of me to make a diagnosis.'

'But you do think it's serious?' she asked shakily.

'It won't affect your life span, Miss Stone.' Only then had he given her a frowning look. 'When I was asked to see you I hadn't realised who you were. I saw you in a play at the Carlton Theatre, but I didn't connect your name with the one I was given.'

'My stage name is Julia Stornaway,' she had explained.

'Ah. If I had known it was you, I would have tried to fit you in earlier.'

Instead of being flattered, she had been angry to find him susceptible to the glamour of show business. As if reading her thoughts, he had smiled. 'You have a rare talent, Miss Stone, and your time away from the stage is a loss to many people.'

'Everyone's illness is a loss—if only to the person who is ill.'

He had taken the point instantly. 'I wouldn't have put someone else off in order to see you more quickly.

Had you come earlier, it would have been during my free time.'

'I see.' She had gone pink. 'I'm sorry.'

He set down his pen. 'Go home, Miss Stone, and pack your things. My secretary will tell Matron to expect you.'

'I didn't know hospital beds were so easy to come by.'

'They aren't.' He rose to escort her to the door. 'I'll be in to see you later this evening.'

His visit to the hospital had been brief, and he was accompanied by his assistant.

'I'll see you in a week's time, Miss Stone,' he had said, placing a firm hand on hers. 'Relax and do everything Dr Meadows tells you. He's nearly as good as I am.'

The young doctor had looked at his superior with an admiration that bordered on idolatry. 'If I ever get to be a quarter as good as you, sir, I'll be satisfied.'

'In medicine and surgery, one should never be satisfied.' Damon Masters' gentle tone had softened his comment, but Juliet remembered it frequently during the following week.

The tests ordered for her were varied. Some only required an injection, but for others she was linked up to machines that looked as if they came from the next century.

Perry had visited her on the first two nights, laden with fruit and flowers and the latest novels. Then for three days he had been too busy, though he had spoken to her on the telephone and promised to see her on Friday.

'It's hell not having you around,' he had confessed. 'Each time I watch Lilah playing your part, I could strangle her!'

She almost told him this was not the impression he had given the last time she had seen him with Lilah, but she bit back the words. Most men would succumb to the Lilahs of this world.

'If anyone can help me, Dr Masters can,' she said instead. 'I'm sure I'll be back on stage soon.'

'So am I,' Perry averred with emotion. 'Be a brave girl and I'll visit you tomorrow after the theatre.'

'That'll be so late,' she had protested. 'Sister will never let you in.'

'Care to bet on it?'

Remembering Perry's persuasive charm, she had laughed.

On Friday Juliet had the last of her tests. She lay on a metal table which moved and tilted in what seemed to be random jerks, while instruments and lights winked at her from every corner of the room. Dr Masters would have plenty of results to study when he returned to England at the weekend. Knowing he had gone to Doria, she had asked one of the nurses if he had a patient there.

'He did have,' came the answer. 'Three years ago he saved the life of the Sheik's eldest son, and when he was asked to choose any present he liked—regardless of cost—he suggested that the Sheik build a neurological centre that would serve the whole of the Middle East. And that's exactly what the Sheik did. It's incredible when you think of it. Doria is a quarter the size of England, yet because of its oilfields it's one of the richest countries in the world.'

Juliet thought of this now as she smoothed her hair and waited for Perry. She wore her prettiest nightgown and had been lavish with scent. But she was still dissatisfied with her appearance, seeing only the hollows in her thin face and the violet shadows beneath her large eyes.

It was nearly midnight before he arrived; breezing in with pink roses, purple grapes and a bottle of champagne. Her heart thumped loudly and she looked at him wide-eyed.

'Do you have any news about me?' she asked excitedly, staring at the champagne bottle.

For a second he did not understand her, then he looked discomfited.

'Sorry, angel, there's no news about you yet. Dr Masters isn't due back until tomorrow and Clarendon won't be speaking to him till Monday.' He fingered the champagne bottle. 'Actually I brought this to celebrate *my* news. It's something sensational that will affect us both.'

Juliet tried to look expectant, but since becoming ill, all she wanted was her health. Everything else seemed unimportant. Yet to say so to Perry would lessen his pleasure in telling her his news.

'I'm waiting, darling,' she smiled, and held out her hands to him.

Dumping the champagne on the dressing table, he perched on the bed and pulled her close. But his hold on her was brief and he quickly rose and paced the room, too excited by his news to sit still.

'Ciné International have asked me to direct a picture in Hollywood,' he said triumphantly. 'It has a ten-million-dollar budget and I can choose my own cast!'

Juliet was overwhelmed. Ciné International was one of the biggest film companies in the world, and for more than a year Perry had been negotiating with them to direct a low-budget film. Neither had expected an offer like this.

'It's unbelievable!' she gasped.

'But true. This will make my name, Juliet. With the right property and a big star, I'll be made.'

'You already have a great reputation,' she said loyally. 'That's why Ciné made you the offer.'

'Even so it's an incredible one. They've even given me the choice of three best-sellers.' His pace quickened round the room. 'I love the theatre as much as you do, but it does have its limitations. In a picture you can use real effects instead of relying on lighting and back-cloths. I can rehearse until every scene is perfect and——' He stopped as he saw the tears pouring down Juliet's face. 'Angel, what is it?'

'I'm so happy for you,' she sobbed. 'Happy and afraid.'

'There's nothing to be afraid of.' He perched on the bed again and hugged her. 'I won't be a failure, darling. This is just the beginning for us, you wait and see. Now wipe your eyes and stop having gloomy thoughts.'

'I'm sorry.' She was angry with herself for spoiling his pleasure. 'I was just overcome by self-pity. What will happen if I can't go to Hollywood with you? If I have to stay here for treatment?'

'We'll worry about that when it happens. But even if you do have to stay behind for a while, it won't be the end of the world. We can talk to each other on the telephone and——'

'But I want to be with you.' She began to cry again. Perry did not like tears, but she could not stop them, and all the sadness and fear which she had hidden from him in the past weeks suddenly spilled over.

'You need a glass of champagne,' he said. 'It's the best pick-you-up in the world.'

The cork popped and liquid foamed into the two

glasses that he produced from a raffia basket. He handed her a brimming goblet and held the other to his lips.

'A toast to our future, my darling. To success and fame.'

'And to health,' she added shakily. 'If you don't have that, nothing else matters.'

'That goes without saying,' he said, and drained his glass.

It was nearly one before he went, leaving behind an empty bottle of champagne, flowers already beginning to droop through lack of water, and hothouse grapes whose bloom was turning to moisture.

'I won't be able to see you tomorrow,' had been his parting words. 'Carl Forburg—Ciné's Vice-President—is flying in from Los Angeles to see me, but I'll try to make it on Sunday.'

'Don't forget to phone and let me know what happens,' Juliet pleaded. 'Otherwise I'll discharge myself from here and come after you.'

'You'll do nothing of the sort, darling girl. I want you to be completely well before you leave here—even if you have to stay for another month.'

She thought of this as the night slowly ticked away and she remained obstinately wide awake. She was too full of champagne she had not wanted and thoughts she did not like. Perry had known of Ciné's offer several days ago, yet he had not told her until tonight. Had he been worried at the way she would react to it? Did he too have a premonition that her illness was not going to disappear overnight?

If only Dr Masters were here to reassure her! She sat up and switched on the bedside lamp, hoping the light would chase away her despondency. But all it did was bring the champagne bottle into focus again and remind her that the news which Perry had come here to celebrate would make their temporary parting inevitable.

'Help me, God,' she prayed. 'Please let Dr Masters make me well.'

CHAPTER FOUR

JULIET kept telling herself that Damon Masters would be too tired from his long flight, and have too many things to catch up with after his absence, to spare time to see her during the weekend. Yet from Saturday afternoon she was keyed up for his visit, and when Sunday arrived and he had still not put in an appearance, she was deeply disappointed.

He had made such an effort to get her into hospital at short notice, and had been so charming to her that she had been sure he was taking a special interest in her. His absence now showed she had been wrong, and she was wryly amused for having misjudged his attitude.

She was not normally a conceited girl, and realised that Perry's absence this weekend had made her focus on Dr Masters; as if the specialist's care for her would compensate for Perry's casualness. Yet Perry cared too. He loved her and wanted to marry her. It was foolish to read more into his absence than a natural abhorrence of sickness.

Unbidden, she remembered Dr Masters' cool sympathy when she had collapsed at his feet in Harley Street and he had carried her into his consulting room. But care of the sick was his life's work—unlike Perry, who was concerned with the glitter of a makebelieve world, where pain was only simulated for a performance and discarded when the show was over.

Knowing this, Juliet had not minded his staying

away yesterday, and had even understood when he had
rung this morning to say he was still tied up with Carl
Forburg.

'How soon does he want you to go to Hollywood?'
she had asked.

'He'd like me to be there yesterday.' Perry sounded
elated. 'The Carlton management have agreed to re-
lease me, so it's only a question of finalising my contract with Ciné.'

'I wish we could get married before you go. Then
I'd join you as soon as Dr Masters discharged me.'

'You can still do that, angel. But I don't want to
marry you while you're in hospital. I want to stand at
the altar and watch you walk up the aisle towards me.'

'Do you really?' She had been moved by the picture
his words painted. 'I thought you'd want to get married in a register office.'

'That shows how little you know me.' The Irish in
his voice was very apparent. 'It's a healthy wife as well
as a beautiful one that I'll be taking, not a pale elf of
a girl.'

'I *will* be well for you,' she whispered. 'Only wait for
me.'

'There's no doubt of that, my angel. But Mr Forburg
won't wait for me, so I must go.'

'Will you be in to see me later?'

'If I'm free.'

He had hung up before she could say any more, and
she had known instinctively that she would not be seeing him today. At six o'clock the nurse came in with
her supper. On the whole the food was palatable, but
Juliet had little appetite for it. She was too anxious
about her future to think of anything as mundane as
eating.

'Dr Masters won't be pleased to hear you're leaving your food,' the nurse told her.

Juliet shrugged and pushed the tray away, and the nurse picked it up and went out. Juliet drew down the white sheet and wished she had asked for the window to be opened wider. It was a sultry evening. All day the sky had been overcast, and now a rumble of thunder presaged a storm. The long russet curtains blew inwards, then settled themselves against the wall, like a maiden lady primly making herself tidy.

Outside in the corridor there was the clatter of trays and crockery as orderlies took round the after-dinner coffee. The door opened—the moving curtains told her that—but she did not bother to turn her head.

'I don't want anything to drink,' she said lethargically. 'And don't nag me any more, because I'm not eating.'

'I wouldn't dream of nagging you.'

Swiftly she swivelled her head, colour flooding her face as she saw Damon Masters. In the small room he looked immense; not only tall but broad too, reminding her once again of a rugger player. She wondered if he had been one, but did not like to ask.

'Good evening,' he went on quietly, and came to stand at the foot of her bed.

On the two occasions she had seen him he had worn a dark suit and white shirt, but tonight he wore grey. Nothing casual or weekendish, but a suit in some very fine material, almost like linen, with a faint check in it. He was slightly bronzed and it made her notice how grey his eyes were.

'I wasn't expecting to see you tonight,' she lied. 'I thought you wouldn't be starting work until tomorrow.'

'I don't have a Monday-to-Friday job.' There was faint humour in his voice. 'I hope you haven't found your stay here too irksome?'

'I didn't expect it to be a holiday. I came here to get well.'

'Yes,' he said, and slipped one hand into the pocket of his jacket.

He kept the other on the rail at the bottom of her bed. His hand was beautifully shaped, with long flexible fingers devoid of rings, and a supple wrist on which she could glimpse a few dark hairs. She glanced away from it quickly. She did not want to see him as a man. He was her specialist, the medical eminence who was going to make her well. He could not be a man, with a man's weaknesses. Her eyes moved up to his face, noting the finely cut mouth and straight, no-nonsense nose, the thick eyebrows that curved precisely above his eyes; steady eyes that met hers without wavering. She felt herself relax. He did not look as if he understood the meaning of the word weakness, so strong and confident did he seem.

'I've had the results of your tests,' he said quietly. 'Do you want it wrapped up or straight from the shoulder?'

Her heart started to thump. The very question implied something unpleasant to follow. She tried to speak, but her mouth was too dry and she moistened her lips.

'I'll give it to you straight,' he went on, before she could say anything. 'I think it's best for you that way.' His eyes still held hers. 'You are suffering from a rare form of nerve damage—so rare that there have only been a dozen reported cases in England in the last five years. Until two years ago we didn't even know what caused it, but now we do have some idea, though we still haven't found a cure.'

She swallowed nervously. 'Will I . . . how much worse will I get?'

'Possibly a little more shaky on your legs, though I can't be sure. What I *am* sure of is that you won't get better spontaneously. There is no known cure, Miss Stone. You must learn to live with it.'

She drew a deep breath and let it out slowly. 'You really have thrown it to me straight from the shoulder!'

'I believe you can take it.'

'I have no option.'

'Cry if you wish,' he said.

'You wouldn't like it if I did.'

'It wouldn't disturb me. But tears won't change the situation.'

'Nothing will,' she said bitterly.

'You should try to count that as a point in its favour.'

'In its favour?' Disbelievingly she stared at him.

'It means it won't get worse,' he explained. 'There are countless numbers of my patients who would give ten years of their lives to know that.'

She was silent. Her desire to cry ebbed, and she felt surprisingly calm.

'Thank you for putting it that way, Dr Masters. It makes things bearable.'

'That was the intention.' His quiet voice held a shade of brusqueness. 'Having accepted that fact, you must now decide how best to live your life. There are certain things you shouldn't do, but many that you still can, providing you take precautions.'

'Like holding on to the banisters when I walk up

and down stairs, and not carrying hot liquid in case my
legs give way and I scald myself. Nor should I try to
beat the lights when I cross the road, in case I collapse
halfway across.'

'Exactly.' Dr Masters smiled. It lessened his gravity
remarkably, and made him look almost boyish. 'The
best way of coping with your condition is to learn to
live with it.' He leaned one broad shoulder against the
wall nearest the bed. The white paintwork threw his
black hair into relief and made his skin look more
deeply bronzed. 'Matron says you've had a lot of
visitors since you've been here, and that you've kept
extremely cheerful.'

'I'm an actress,' Juliet said wryly. 'Some of the cast
came to see me, and also Perry—Peregrine Langdon,
the director of the play I was in.'

'Your fiancé,' Dr Masters said, and seeing her sur-
prise that he should know this, added: 'I spoke to Dr
Clarendon last night and he said he would be calling
Mr Langdon to tell him the results.'

'Perry's very anxious to know. He's going to Hollywood shortly and I—we would like to be together.'

'There's no reason why you shouldn't be.'

'You mean I'm free to leave the hospital?' In her
earnestness she leaned forward. The top of her nightdress slipped and the curve of her breasts was visible.
She felt Dr Masters' eyes upon them, but they remained blank.

'I've already explained to you, Miss Stone, that providing you take precautions, you can lead a normal
life.'

'What's normal for one person isn't normal for another. If I never know when I'm going to fall down, I

can't appear on stage, can I? Not unless I take the part of an invalid.'

He frowned, as if this aspect of her life had not occurred to him. But then why should it? she thought irritably. She was merely a patient he could not cure; though luckily one who was not going to die from her illness or get much worse.

'You weren't lying to me, were you?' she asked abruptly. 'I won't suddenly deteriorate, will I?'

'I do not lie to my patients, Miss Stone.' He came to stand beside the bed. 'You're a gifted actress and it would be a great pity if you gave up your career. Have you thought of film work? If you fall down they can always re-shoot the scene.'

'Or shoot me,' she smiled, and shook her head. 'If I were already known as a screen actress there might be a chance of my continuing, but as far as the film world is concerned I'm an unknown, and no one will take a chance on a sick actress when there are so many healthy ones available.'

'That's defeatist talk. I'm sure Mr Langdon wouldn't agree with you.'

Juliet wished Perry were here. She was beginning to feel lightheaded and knew it was due to both fear and relief. Relief that she wasn't going to become an invalid, and fear of what Perry's reaction had been when he had learned she would never fully recover.

'Would you like me to speak to Mr Langdon?' the specialist asked. 'I know Dr Clarendon has spoken to him, but I'll gladly talk to him myself if you think it will reassure him.'

She gave him a grateful smile. 'I don't think that will be necessary, thank you. But if it is, I'll let you know.'

'Good. In that case I'll leave you to rest.'

He put his hand lightly on the top of her head. It was a gesture of reassurance, though when he spoke, his words surprised her.

'You're a brave young woman, Julia Stornaway.'

'Please don't call me by that name,' she begged. 'It belongs to my past. From now on I'm Juliet Stone—nothing else.'

'Nothing else?' A slight smile lifted the corners of his mouth. 'I happen to think it's a great deal.'

Without another word he left her, but Juliet was too concerned over Perry to consider his final comment. Why had he pretended not to know the results of her tests when he had spoken to her this morning? And knowing it, how could he have stayed away from her today, no matter how important Carl Forburg was?

Restlessly she shifted in the bed, not liking what her intelligence told her yet determined to face it. The discovery that her illness was not curable must have come as a great shock to him, and he probably needed time to come to terms with it. Nor had he realised that Dr Masters would see her today and tell her the truth.

She debated whether to call Perry and tell him that she knew, then decided against it. It would be better for both of them if they had time to absorb the shock of it before they spoke to each other.

On Monday morning Dr Masters' houseman came in to tell her that two more tests had been ordered for her.

'It means you'll be our guest for a little longer,' he joked. 'But there's no reason for you to stay in bed. You may put on your dressing gown and pretend you're staying at a health farm.'

She smiled to show she appreciated his effort to

lighten her mood, but knew that only when she saw Perry and was reassured of his love would she feel like genuinely smiling.

Gingerly she got out of bed, gaining more confidence as she wandered around the room without collapsing. She felt so normal that she almost wondered if the whole thing was a bad dream from which she would awaken. But as she turned to reach for her housecoat, her knees buckled and she fell to the floor with a thump that brought tears of pain to her eyes.

'Damn, damn, damn!' she cried, and remained where she was, knowing it would take a moment for her legs to recover their mobility.

Sometimes the weakness disappeared quickly, at other times it took longer. Was this what Dr Masters meant when he said it might get worse, or did he mean that the frequency of the attacks might increase? She must remember to ask him. Yet either way it made no difference. She would never be normal and she must accept that fact.

Cautiously she moved. Her legs were no longer numb and she clambered up and went to the dressing-table. Perry was certain to call in some time this morning, and she arranged her hair in the way he liked best: pulled away from her face into a loop on her neck, and held there by a wide tortoiseshell comb. The style accentuated the thinness of her face and made one aware of the fragile curve of her neck and shoulders, visible beneath her blue silk wrap. The wrap was the same colour as Perry's eyes and he had bought it for her because he had said it would remind her of him each time she wore it. She put a trembling hand to her forehead. As if she needed anything to remind her of Perry!

Resisting the urge to call him, she sat in an arm-chair by the window. Was he at the theatre or still in his apartment? It would depend how long he had talked with Carl Forburg, and she hoped all had gone well for him.

A nurse came in with an enormous sheaf of flowers. Through the cellophane Juliet glimpsed dozens of orchids.

'Aren't they magnificent?' the nurse smiled. 'Would you like me to undo them for you and put them in water?'

At Juliet's nod she ripped off the cellophane and tenderly lifted out the blooms. There were twelve sprays, each one two feet long and each one thick with mauve and pink orchids.

'I never knew they grew like that,' Juliet said.

'Nor did I. I thought they grew in a corsage, ready to be pinned on a dress. I'll fetch some big vases. They're so gorgeous they need to be properly displayed.'

The nurse was half-way through the door when she rummaged in the pocket of her apron and handed Juliet an envelope. 'Silly of me—I nearly forgot the letter that came with it. Not that you'll need to know the name of the man who sent you these!'

Juliet tore open the envelope. The nurse was right. Only one man was capable of sending her such an extravagant bouquet.

'My darling Juliet,' Perry wrote, 'I was distraught when Dr Clarendon told me the results of your tests. I never expected anything like this. But at least you won't die from your illness, so we should be grateful on that score alone. But when I think of the wonderful career you were on the verge of having, and of your brilliant talent which you will never be able to use, I can weep—for you, for me, for the countless number of people who will never have the joy of watching you act. Darling angel, if only I could give you my own strength! But unfortunately I can do nothing....'

There was more in the same vein, and it was only when she came to the second page that she reached the crux of the letter.

Perry did not want to marry her.

He still loved her, he said, but he was not a martyr, and to marry her knowing she would never achieve her full potential was martyrdom indeed. Because of this it was best for them to part; best too for them to do it without a face-to-face confrontation which would be painful for them both.

'I'm leaving for Hollywood today. Carl wants me there at once and there's no point in delaying. You know my motto, angel. When the rainbow shines for you, straddle it before it fades. Please don't feel bitter towards me. I know you will, but I hope that when the hurt has gone you will understand my reasons. I love you, dearest girl, but I love you the way you were. To watch you stumble around would break my heart.'

'But you don't care about breaking *mine*!' Juliet cried aloud, and flung the letter to the floor. How could she love a man and know him so little? Had she blinded herself to his egocentricity, to his conceit, to his shallowness where human relationships were concerned? Yet she had to admit he had often said he could not tolerate stress—be it from people or situations. That was why everyone enjoyed working with him. They knew that in a Perry Langdon production there would be no arguments; because if you did not do things his way, you were out.

Until this moment she had seen such an attitude as

a virtue; now she saw it as a Peter Pan characteristic. Perry wanted everything to be ideal. *His* ideal. Life must be his personal fairy tale, where everything was sweetness and light, and if he saw the light fading and the sweetness growing sour, then he would—to use his own words—straddle the first rainbow that came his way and be wafted off to a better land.

It was a long while before Juliet's tears subsided and she was able to think coherently. She might be dead inside, but she had to carry on living. Which brought her to the salient question of what she could do. The obvious choice was secretarial, except that she did not have enough money to take a secretarial course. Foolishly she had spent every penny she had earned: buying the clothes Perry liked her to wear, finding an expensive flat that he would enjoy visiting, plying him with the delicacies he enjoyed eating.

He had been generous too, of course. Bottles of French perfume, the occasional haute couture dress and a constant stream of fripperies had come her way. But when all was said and done she was left with nothing. Yet it was not the meagreness of her bank account that set her crying afresh, but the barrenness of her future. With a little moan she buried her head in her hands.

A nurse, coming in later with her luncheon tray, found her sitting motionless beside the bed, staring into space. But she made no comment until she returned to collect the tray and found the food untouched.

'Aren't you feeling well, Miss Stone? Or didn't you like the food?'

'I'm not hungry,' said Juliet flatly.

'You should still eat something. Would you like an omelette?'

'No, thank you.' As the nurse went to pick up the tray, Juliet pointed to the orchids. 'Please take them. I know you like them.'

'Take them? Oh, you can't mean that!'

'I do. Take them all.'

Silently the nurse did as she was told and Juliet fought back the tears. She must get used to the knowledge that Perry had walked out on her; must accept that from now on she had to make her own life. She picked up his letter and started to re-read it, but before she was half-way through, her tears returned.

A slight cough was her first indication that she was not alone. Lifting her head, she saw Dr Masters. Embarrassed, she quickly wiped her eyes.

'I'm sorry,' she gulped. 'I—I guess I'm not as brave as you first thought.'

He perched his tall frame on the edge of the dressing-table. One long leg touched the floor and he swung the other idly. 'You've had some bad news, haven't you?'

'How do you know?'

'The nurse told me you hadn't eaten your lunch and when I saw the orchids on the floor outside and she said you didn't want them. . . .' He gave a faintly ironic smile. 'No woman gives away such magnificent flowers without having a reason.'

'Yes.' Juliet could not bring herself to say more, and averted her head, ashamed to let him see her puffy face. She heard him move towards her and apathetically turned to him again.

'You dropped this on the floor,' he said, holding out Perry's letter.

She looked at it and shuddered. 'Read it, Dr Masters. You may have some fatherly advice to give me.'

'Are you sure you want me to read it?'

'There's nothing secret in it.'

Her voice cracked and once more she turned away. Behind her she heard the paper rustle and knew that Dr Masters had gone to sit on the edge of the bed. There was silence for a while, then he spoke.

'I don't suppose you will agree with me, Miss Stone, but you should regard your illness as an ill wind that blew some good.'

She looked astonished and he went on:

'It's shown you the man your fiancé is.'

'I understand how he feels,' she said shakily. 'He hates illness.'

'More than he loves you, it seems.'

She coloured. 'I don't expect you to understand. You're used to suffering. Your whole life is devoted to sick people. You don't know what that sort of thing can do to a man like Perry. He's an artist. He needs happiness around him.'

'We'd all like that. But the sun isn't dimmed by a few shadows.'

'My illness is more than a shadow,' she cried. 'It's total blackness!'

'Only if you make it so.'

'I didn't make it anything,' she cried, and burst into another storm of weeping. 'I wish I was dead. I wish I could go to sleep and never wake up!'

'Stop it!' The voice was quiet, but the words held such authority that she tried to stifle her sobs.

'How dare you cry over such a worthless man?' he demanded. 'He isn't fit to touch your shoes, let alone marry you.'

'I love him.'

'You love a false image. You don't see it now, but one day you will.' He went to the door. 'Cry as much as you like for the rest of the day, but I shall expect you to be in control of yourself by tomorrow. You're brave and strong and I won't let you be destroyed by a —by anyone.'

In a gesture that was almost violent, he opened the door and walked out.

CHAPTER FIVE

DAMON MASTERS knew, as he woke up next morning, exactly what he was going to say to Juliet Stone when he saw her that afternoon.

He didn't know when he had made the decision, but he was certain it had not come upon him suddenly. His mind was too well disciplined to let impulsive ideas take over. At least he had always assumed so, though since meeting Juliet he was no longer sure.

It was disquieting to think that a girl who was completely unaware of him as a man had been able to turn his life upside down. He could recall every detail about her; the exact colour of her hair: rich brown with russet lights; her huge sherry-brown eyes which these last few days had been dark as the heart of a sunflower. Damn it, he was even getting poetical! But it was hard not to be, when every fibre of his body tingled with desire for her.

But why Juliet Stone? What was so special about her that made him want her and no one else? Had he been easily swayed by women, he could have understood his behaviour more easily. But he had always been immune to feminine charms. He admired beauty and had occasionally drunk at its fountain, but he had always extricated himself before drinking too deeply. Yet here he was, plunging willingly into deep water, even though there was a strong chance of his drowning.

A wry smile twisted his mouth. It was a mannerism

that gave him a sardonic look which was alien to his nature. But then his looks had always belied his character; a fact which had made his life difficult from an early age.

'A big chap like you has to be good at sport,' the games master at his prep school had said, astonished to learn that Masters preferred to spend his leisure enjoying the minutiae of pond life rather than playing on the rugger field.

Inevitably the games master had won the day and Damon had played rugger and excelled at it, as he excelled at everything he did, whether he enjoyed it or not. Success came to him as naturally as breathing. His father had been the same, and so had his grandfather; both of them eminent surgeons. The Masters men always reached the top, whatever they did.

When he was fifteen, Damon's interest had turned to medicine. He had worked hard because he had loved it, and because everything else—friendship, women, hobbies—was insignificant by comparison.

Twice he had nearly married, but on both occasions he had realised that his feeling for the woman was lukewarm compared with his feelings for his work. He knew that his continuing bachelor status was a source of anxiety to his mother and his three sisters, but in the last few years they had resigned themselves to it and stopped their matchmaking. How astonished they would be with him if his ploy to get Juliet worked!

Why then had Juliet Stone made such an impact on him? The storm she raised was so overwhelming that no sane reason could account for it. Were he given to mysticism he might have believed they had met in another incarnation and had shared a life together. That Juliet herself had no such feelings about him was obvious. It was a good thing too, for had she shown the slightest interest in him, God knows what would have happened to his self-control. As it was, each time he saw her, so thin and pale, he was hard pressed not to pull her into his arms and tell her she had nothing to fear as long as he was alive to take care of her.

'Fool!'

The word came from him like an expletive and he sat up and reached for the silver coffee pot. In planning what to say to her this afternoon, he was closing his mind to the way she regarded him. All he knew was that he had to keep her in his life, no matter on what terms.

Belatedly he wished there was someone to whom he could talk about the wisdom of what he planned. But his family would think him mad, and the few men with whom he could discuss such a personal matter would see it only in sexual terms and suggest a quick affair to get it out of his system. But he knew that the emotion Juliet Stone aroused in him was far deeper than physical desire, though that in itself was strong enough. Indeed its strength had amazed him, showing him the frailty of what he had believed to be his iron control.

'I'm behaving like a lovesick schoolboy,' he muttered. 'I can't be logical about her, and there's an end to it. If my plan works, I'll be the luckiest man alive, and if it doesn't, I'll at least have the satisfaction of knowing I tried.'

Draining his coffee at a gulp, he flung back the fine cotton sheet that covered him and went lithe-footed to the bathroom.

His rounds that morning were a penance that had to be put behind him as quickly as possible, though he was careful to show none of his tension to his patients, with whom he was uniformly courteous.

He was booked to lunch with a colleague who wished to discuss a complex new technique that had lately been developed in America, and he had to concentrate hard in order to answer the queries that this raised. It was such an effort for him that he knew he would never again be impatient with the lovesick junior doctors who occasionally came his way. Tolerance, he thought wryly, was being taught to him the hard way.

Three-thirty found him striding down the corridor to Juliet's room. He had not warned the Sister on the floor that he was coming, though medical etiquette required that a nurse be present when a doctor saw a patient.

His hand was on the door of her room when a nurse hurried forward, twittering anxiously in case he had been looking for someone.

'I want to talk to Miss Stone privately,' he informed her, and stepped smartly inside before she could reply.

Juliet was sitting in an armchair, looking almost the way he had left her yesterday, except that her face was no longer tear-stained and her eyes, instead of being red-rimmed, were lifeless as those of a doll.

'Hello,' she said, and gave him a meaningless smile, 'I feel a bit of a fraud remaining here. If you can't do any more for me, there's no reason why I shouldn't come in for my tests as an out-patient.'

'I would prefer you to remain here. We need to check your fluid intake.' Her listless acquiescence told him she was still numb from the shock she had received yesterday. 'Do you mind if I sit down and talk to you, Juliet?'

He saw that his use of her first name had surprised her, but he had decided it was impossible to call her Miss Stone and say what he wanted to say. Anyway, she would be even more surprised in a few minutes.

'I want to talk to you on a personal level,' he went on. 'I've given a great deal of thought to what I'm going to say.'

Damon almost added that he had thought of nothing else since their first meeting, but knew that if he revealed the intensity of his feelings, he would scare her off. All she was looking for—whether she knew it or not—was a haven where she could relax; a haven which he was willing to provide.

'Have you made any plans for the future, Juliet?'

'No. I shall talk to someone at the labour exchange and see if I qualify for a disability pension.'

'It's wrong to think of yourself as an invalid.'

'I can hardly be classified as normal.'

'You *are* normal,' he said impatiently. 'If you weren't, I wouldn't be prepared to ask you to ... to put forward the suggestion I have to make.'

Her head tilted. 'Are you asking me to come and work for you, Dr Masters?'

'I'm asking you to be my wife.'

There had not been much colour in her face when he had come into the room, but what little there was faded completely as she absorbed what he said.

'I know it's come as a surprise to you,' he went on, 'but I haven't had time to lead up to it. Events have moved quickly for both of us.'

'Very quickly.' Her voice was a thin thread of sound, like cotton about to break. 'I take it you're not—you're not saying you love me?'

'No,' he lied, 'I'm not. But you need some occupation that will give you security—and I need a wife.'

'You appear to have managed very well without one.'

'Circumstances change.' He folded his arms across his chest and sought for a way of convincing her that if she accepted him, she would be doing him a favour. 'Until now, my work has given me every satisfaction I need. That doesn't mean I'm a misogynist; I like women and I have known several fairly well, but I've never loved any of them sufficiently to marry. Three years ago I treated the eldest son of Sheik Quima, who is the ruler of Doria.'

'One of the nurses told me about it. The Sheik built a clinic for you, didn't he?'

'Yes. And that happens to have a bearing on my proposal. The Quima Neurological Clinic has just opened and the Sheik wishes me to go there for a year to supervise it and to make sure it follows my own method of working.'

'Isn't it difficult for you to leave London?'

'It presents problems,' he admitted, 'but not in-surmountable ones.'

'You wouldn't let anything stop you if you wanted to do something.'

The half smile which accompanied her comment told him he had her full attention, and also that she had some insight into his character.

'There's one problem I haven't been able to over-come,' he continued. 'The majority of my patients will be Muslims, and as you know, a woman has to be at death's door before she'll allow a male doctor to examine her. If that doctor also happens to be un-married, it's highly likely she would prefer to die.'

'Surely not in this day and age?'

'I'm afraid so. Don't make the mistake of thinking

that progress knows no barriers. Religion is still the greatest barrier of all. That's why I need a wife to accompany me to Doria. When we return to England we can end the contract—or continue with it—depending on how we feel by then.'

'You make it sound so businesslike,' she said flatly.

'It's a business proposition.'

'A very unusual one.'

'The circumstances are unusual for both of us.'

Juliet bit her lip. 'Why me, Dr Masters? Surely you know lots of women who are far more suitable—women with your own background and education.'

He longed to tell her she was everything he wanted, but knew it would be fatal. Yet he had to say something to disarm her, and cursed himself for not anticipating such a question.

'The sort of woman you would consider suitable for me, is not the sort to be interested in a temporary marriage.'

'How do you know *I* won't try to cling to you?'

'Would you?' he asked whimsically.

'No. Nor will cling now. I'm sorry, Dr Masters, but I can't marry you. The whole thing is too cold-blooded.'

'Should I have pretended that I fell in love with you at first sight? That when I saw you walk across the stage at the Carlton Theatre I knew you were the only girl for me?'

She gave a genuine smile. 'If you'd said that, I would have thought you a liar.'

'Then since I haven't lied and am being honest with you, why penalise me? I'm offering you a job for a year—longer if we both wish it.'

'How can one marry for a year?' she protested. 'It's making a mockery of the whole thing!'

'Many people marry just to get another nationality,' he replied. 'I'm asking you to marry me so that I can help to organise a Clinic in a part of the world that's in urgent need of medical aid. You wouldn't only be doing *me* a favour, you would be helping hundreds of women—probably thousands. You have nothing to lose, Juliet. I won't make any physical demands on you.'

'But I'm ill,' she cried. 'What sort of wife can I be if I never know when I'm going to fall down?'

'I don't lead an active social life,' he answered. 'Having someone who wants a peaceful existence will be a great help to me.'

'You have everything worked out, haven't you?'

'Is that wrong?'

'Calculating, more than wrong.' She coloured. 'I'm sorry if that sounds rude.'

'Don't apologise for your honesty. I understand what you mean.'

'I still don't think I can do it. I'm flattered that you asked me, but I.... It wouldn't be right.'

'Are you still hoping Mr Langdon will——'

'No,' she interrupted. 'It has nothing to do with Perry.'

'Then don't dismiss my proposal. Think it over.'

'I won't change my mind, Dr Masters. There's no——' She stopped as a nurse came into the room holding out a newspaper.

'Sorry,' the girl said, disconcerted to see such a distinguished consultant sitting beside her patient. 'I didn't know you were here, Dr Masters.'

Damon nodded and the nurse dropped the paper on Juliet's lap and went out.

'Please think over my proposal,' he repeated as the

door closed. 'Then we'll talk about it again.'

He rose and, in doing so, glanced at the newspaper. Juliet followed his eyes and the photograph half-way down the page caught her attention. With an indrawn breath she picked up the paper. Quietly Damon stepped behind her and looked at it too. He saw a narrow-faced man with puckish features, standing beside a voluptuous-looking brunette. They were both in casual denims and looked confidently happy. The caption beneath the picture explained why: Peregrine Langdon and Lilah Rhodes were flying to Hollywood where Langdon was to direct and Lilah to star in a multi-million-dollar production of one of the latest best-selling novels.

'My dear,' Damon said gently, and placed his hand on Juliet's shoulder. He felt her body shaking and could cheerfully have strangled the man who was the cause of it.

'What a fool I am!' she whispered. 'I thought it was because of my illness. But it was Lilah all along. Perry wanted her instead of me.'

'Then it's a good thing you found out now instead of later. It would have been worse if you were married to him.'

'It might not have happened if we'd been married.'

'A man who deserts his fiancée when she's ill can also do the same to his wife.' Damon was no longer able to hide his anger. 'Langdon isn't worthy of loving.'

'One can't love to order.'

'But one can put order into one's life. Remember that, Juliet.'

She raised shadowed eyes to his. 'You make everything sound so easy, Dr Masters.'

'That's what I'm trying to do.' He bent forward. 'Think over my proposal.'

'There's no need. As you said, it's like taking a job.' Her lids lowered and thick lashes marked her cheeks. 'If it will help you, then I—I will marry you.'

Triumph filled him, but he was careful to hide it. He stepped away from her, afraid that if he didn't he would pull her into his arms.

'You won't regret it,' he said formally. 'I'll get a licence and make all the arrangements. Leave everything to me.'

Swiftly he went out, then leaned for a moment against the wall before striding down to the consulting room that he used here. Without hesitation he dialled Western Union, then gave the name and address of Sheik Quima in Doria.

'Plans changed,' he dictated. 'Agreeable to oversee Clinic for one year. Will discuss arrangements with your Ambassador here.'

He replaced the receiver and stared at it thoughtfully. It was too late to wonder if he had done the right thing. He had built a bridge and crossed it. Only time would tell whether the bridge would stand up to the ebb and flow of the currents that would pass beneath it in the next twelve months.

CHAPTER SIX

JULIET paused on the threshold of the sliding doors and listened to the hum of the air-conditioning. Then she slid the door aside and stepped out, swiftly closing the door behind her. In a climate like this it was essential not to let the heat enter the house.

The sunshine was overpowering, yet just as one thought one could no longer bear it, a cool breeze blew in from the sea, bringing with it a freshness that was in marked contrast to the dry, dust-laden air.

'It isn't dust,' Damon had told her. 'It's sand. And you only get it when there's a strong wind blowing in from the desert. When there's no wind, the air is wonderfully clear.'

He was right, of course; he invariably was. That was something which two months of marriage had taught her. They had married three weeks after her discharge from hospital. Damon had insisted on it, almost as if he were afraid she would change her mind. Remembering it, Juliet smiled wryly. Bereft of Perry and with no hope of immediate work, she had been unlikely to turn down the gift horse which Damon offered: a contract of marriage to one of the world's most eminent neurologists. Even when their marriage ended she would be left with a tidy sum of money, since Damon insisted on giving her a monthly allowance as payment for the job she was doing.

She wandered across the small lawn, kept brilliantly green by constant watering, and settled in a wicker lounger. It was hard to think of her marriage as a job, and if she weren't still pining for Perry she would have found it difficult to complain about her present situation. Unfortunately it gave her too much time to brood, and she wished she could find something to do.

Cooking was out of the question. Damon ate sparingly, but he liked his food to be exceptionally well prepared, and Juliet knew she could never meet his standards. Had the marriage been a permanent one she would have taken a cookery course when they returned to England, but by then Damon might decide he no longer required a wife. She sighed and wished she felt closer to him, yet knew that if he made any move in this direction himself, she would be afraid.

When he had first put forward his astonishing proposal he had said they might mutually decide not to part when he left Doria. At the time she had barely taken this in, but of late she had thought of it frequently, and was curious to know if he still felt the same. He was always charming to her, but she sensed a reserve between them, as if he were afraid of letting himself go. Such reserve might be part of his character, but she had no means of knowing. Had they been in England she might have learned more about him by talking to his family, whom she had met for the first time a day before their wedding.

His mother and three sisters had all seemed delighted that Damon was finally taking the plunge, and they were especially pleased that he was marrying a girl with no medical background.

'We were always worried in case he married a nurse or a doctor,' the youngest sister had confided during a few brief moments alone with Juliet. 'If he had, he would never have relaxed at all. Can't you just see him talking shop when he should be making love?'

Embarrassment had kept Juliet silent, but it had been seen as shyness.

'You're exactly right for Damon,' her new sister-in-law had continued. 'And he obviously dotes on you. I watched him looking at you in the register office. His expression was melting and tender—the way he'd look at a benign tumour!'

'What a ghastly simile!' Juliet had laughed, but when Damon had come towards her shortly afterwards she had watched him surreptitiously. But he had looked at her the way he always did: with dispassionate friendliness.

He was walking towards her now, and she glanced at her wrist watch. It was noon and he would spend the next hour and a half at home, having lunch and a rest before returning to the Clinic.

Since coming here he had worked almost non-stop, relaxing only for half a day each Sunday. Two weeks ago she had noticed how haggard he looked and had been surprised by the concern she felt for him. Pretending that she found it depressing to be left by herself for such long periods, she begged him to stay with her for the whole of each Sunday, and also to lengthen his lunch break. He had complied immediately, but she had found herself wondering if he had worked so hard because he did not want to be with her. Yet the idea was foolish. Had he not liked her, he would never have asked her to come to Doria with him.

Damon took off his jacket and eased himself into a chair beside her. He wore a short-sleeved cream shirt with a tan tie that matched his linen suit. The colour made him look younger than the thirty-seven she knew him to be, though he would have looked younger still had it not been for the silvery flecks at his temples. She tried to imagine his hair completely dark and half shook her head. The touch of silver was distinguished and made him look handsome.

'What have I done wrong?' he asked wryly. 'You're looking at me and shaking your head.'

'I was deciding that I like the grey flecks in your hair.'

'His grey eminence?' he quizzed. 'Do you see me as an old patriarch?'

'I see you as a young one!'

He smiled, showing even white teeth. 'You're very flattering to me all of a sudden. In other women I would suspect it was leading up to a request for something.'

'I have everything I need,' she smiled.

He remained leaning back in his chair, yet gave an impression of tenseness.

'Do you mean that, Juliet? Isn't there the slightest regret for having married me and come out to this Godforsaken hole?'

'No regrets whatever,' she said swiftly. 'And I think it's mean of you to be so unflattering about Doria.'

She glanced across the lush lawn to the larger expanse of their garden, where the grass lay parched and brown beneath an electric blue sky. Beyond the gardens stretched the desert, an undulating expanse of golden sand, where the grains moved only when the wind blew. Behind them lay the capital Kuwan—a bustling modern metropolis with skyscrapers, tall office blocks and gleaming new hotels ranged along the recently built esplanade that bordered the Arabian Sea.

Driving past these hotels and seeing the huge apartment blocks, it was hard to believe that ten years ago ninety per cent of the area had been desert. But as the oil had gushed, the buildings had sprouted, and now there were even government restrictions to watch over dubious land speculators.

'Kuwan's a lovely city,' she added. 'The architecture is excellent and everything is bright and clean.'

'It's a brash and soulless city,' Damon replied, 'though I grant you it has some excellent shops. I bought this shirt in one of them.'

He fingered the silk and, as always, she was aware of his beautifully-shaped hands.

'I didn't know you'd been shopping,' she said.

'I don't work non-stop,' he smiled.

'You might at least have taken me with you when you went into the city.'

'I thought you'd be bored.'

'I could have bought you a tie. It's what most wives do.'

He grinned. 'Heaven spare me from that! I've yet to meet a woman who can choose a tie for a man.'

'There's no problem selecting one for you. It has to be in thick silk in navy, maroon or brown.'

'How dull and conservative I am,' he said dryly.

Deliberately Juliet studied him. He met her look with nonchalance, his grey-green eyes giving away none of his thoughts. A breeze ruffled the back of his hair but did not disturb the smoothness at the front, where the thick strands were brushed away from his high forehead. Two faint lines marked his brow and there was a network of fine lines at the corners of his eyes, more noticeable since he had come to Doria. She was not sure whether it was due to lack of sleep or the habit he had of crinkling his eyes against the sun.

'You're not a bit dull or conservative,' she said.

'You've adjusted to this life as if you've known no other.'

'You mean I don't have bacon and eggs for breakfast each morning?'

She laughed. 'Nor have I heard you complain about the way the Clinic is run. Yet I know you've been furious at some of the things that have happened there.'

'Only because I hate to see expensive equipment maltreated. The Dorians are still so backward,' he said vehemently, 'and the best training can't give them an appreciation of the fragility of some of the machines they're handling. That type of knowledge only comes after years of experience.'

'I know,' she sympathised. 'I once met someone who'd trained Iraqui pilots. He said they were fearless in the air but had no idea how to look after their aircraft. They treated them as if they were expendable.'

'I have the same problem,' Damon muttered. 'But I'm trying to do something about it. I've engaged three technicians from England and I've managed to get hold of an ex-Matron who's agreed to come here for the length of my stay. If *she* can't instil discipline into the Dorian nurses, no one can.'

'I'd be happier if you said you were getting more help for yourself,' Juliet said crisply. 'You work far too hard.'

'I am getting someone,' he replied amiably. 'She's arriving today.'

'Today?' Juliet gaped at him. 'And you did say *she*?'

'Why not? These days it would be more than I dare do to advertise for a man. Besides, Monique is an ex-

cellent surgeon. I knew her when she first qualified—
and she was good then.'

Juliet was curious to know more, but held her
tongue. Weeks ago she had decided never to ask
Damon for an explanation of anything he did. She
heard him give a faint, almost exasperated sigh.

'Don't you want to know about her?' he asked.
'After all, there aren't many women here with whom
you can be friends. Or don't you miss feminine company?'

'Of course I do. I'd love to know more about her, but
I didn't like to ask you.'

'Why not? Do you find me so difficult to talk to?'

'You know I don't.'

'You could have fooled me,' he said shortly.

Astonishment held her captive. Was Damon trying
to pick a quarrel with her?

'I'll get you something cool to drink,' she said
calmly. 'You look tired and hot.'

'And it's making me a bad-tempered devil,' he added.

'You're very good-tempered,' she protested, and rose
quickly.

Without warning her legs gave way and she flung
out her hands. Damon caught her as she collapsed, half
on the grass, half on his lap. With ease he pulled her
completely on to his lap and she rested there, trembling and waiting for her legs to recover their strength.

'That's the first time in three days,' she muttered. 'I
was hoping I'd made a miraculous recovery.'

'It doesn't happen that way.' His voice was rough,
though his hold was gentle.

'It doesn't stop me hoping.'

He said nothing and she fell silent. She tried to
move her legs, but there was no feeling in them yet,

and she had to stay where she was. She was surprised that his lap was comfortable and not bony, and she relaxed again.

'Good,' he said, feeling it. 'You won't be able to walk for a few minutes.'

'Sometimes I get scared I'll never be able to walk again. I know you've told me it won't happen, but....'

'Be quiet!' He pulled her against his chest as if she were a child in need of comfort. One of his hands moved up to rest on top of her head, and he stroked the silky hair.

Juliet had never been so close to him before. He had kissed her in the register office—having explained earlier that he did not wish his family to know his marriage was one of expedience—but they had been surrounded by people and his touch had been perfunctory. But here there was no one to watch them except some soporific insects in the shrubbery. She could hear his heart beating steadily and wondered if it was always as loud as this. His breath came fast and she felt its warmth on her temple. The silk shirt was smooth upon her face and had a delicate scent. Yet it was the scent of Damon himself: a fresh, clean smell that epitomised his whole character for her.

She half raised her head, then instantly regretted it, for she found he had lowered his own to look at her. His eyes were so near that the flecks in them were like tiny green leaves. His lashes were surprisingly long and, seen at such close range, gave him a vulnerable look which she had never before noticed.

'Juliet,' he said huskily, and touched his lips to hers.

It was a gentle kiss whose softness made her more aware of the touch of his mouth. Was this the same mouth that could so often look withdrawn? But there was nothing withdrawn about it now, as it moved over hers with tender insistence. Her lips parted slightly and she put her arms upon his shoulders. Dear Damon, who had rescued her when she had been at her lowest ebb and had shown her unfailing kindness ever since. It did not matter that he only needed her professionally; all she knew was that she could rely on him and that he would not let her down.

As her hold tightened, he rose to his feet and lifted her up in his arms. 'I'd better carry you inside, Juliet. It's unwise to sit out here at midday, even in the shade.'

Disappointment kept her quiet. He had clearly shown her he regretted his loss of control and she was ashamed at the way she had responded to his kiss. Because she did not wish him to read too much into it, she said quickly: 'You can put me down, Damon. I'm sure I can walk.'

Surprisingly he did as she asked, though he gave her a supporting arm until he saw she could stand properly. Then together they went into the house.

'You're very good to me, Damon.' She was still determined to set the record straight. 'I'll never forget how kind you've been.'

'You're making it sound like an epilogue,' he replied, 'and we haven't yet got through the prologue.'

Glancing at him, she saw his mouth was tilted at the corners in his habitually whimsical expression, as if only by finding the world an amusing place could he bear to remain in it.

'We've been married for two months, Damon. We're well into the first act.'

'Are you anxious for the play to end?'

'No. I'm happy with you, and grateful for all you've done for me.'

'We're both helping each other, Juliet. Don't use the word gratitude.'

They didn't talk much during lunch, and as soon as it was over Damon left for the airport to meet his new surgeon. Juliet wondered if he would have done the same if a man was arriving. Because she still felt shy with him after their kiss she did not put the question into words, nor did she remind him that he had promised to tell her more about the woman. He would do so when the mood suited him.

As always Juliet spent part of the afternoon indoors, only venturing out when the burning heat lessened. During her first few weeks here she had kept the air-conditioning at its coldest level, until a continual snuffle in her nose prompted Damon to suggest she keep the house more compatible with the outside temperature.

'To go from one extreme to another is harmful,' he had explained. 'I suggest you let me regulate the thermostats. It won't be as cold as you'd like in the house, but neither of us will then run the risk of dying of pneumonia.'

As always he had been proved right, and though the interior of the house was warm by English standards, it was cool compared with the heat outside.

At four-thirty she drove to the Clinic, taken there by the dusky-skinned young man who acted as chauffeur-cum-houseboy. Damon refused to let her drive, explaining that since she never knew when her legs would give way, she might lose control of the car. In moments of deepest despondency Juliet felt this might not be a bad thing for her, but she kept the thought to herself.

Most afternoons she went for a drive. It gave her a

change of scene and helped to pass the time, though as she had said to Damon earlier that day, she had no desire to do any personal shopping. Part of the reason was her reluctance to spend her money. She still felt guilty at accepting it from Damon, but knew it was her only security against a time when she would be alone again.

'Does Madam wish to call upon her husband?' Ali asked, slowing the car as the five-storey Clinic came into sight.

'No, thanks,' Juliet said swiftly. 'I'm sure the doctor is too busy to be disturbed.'

This question and answer was a regular ritual whenever they drove anywhere near the Clinic, and she knew Ali was astonished that she did not wish to show off her relationship with her husband, for whom he himself would willingly have died. Indeed Damon's word was law to him, and he had confided shyly that as the doctor allowed his wife to appear with her face uncovered in public, he would do the same when he married.

Ali slowed down the car and Juliet was about to tell him to drive more quickly, when she saw the tall, upright figure of her husband stepping out of a dark limousine. A woman followed him, but she was too far away for Juliet to see her clearly. It was only Damon's height that had singled him out. As if her thoughts were a signal, he turned and stared in the direction of her car, recognising its distinctive pale blue colour.

'The master has seen us,' Ali said happily, and drew to a stop.

Damon turned to his companion for an instant and then came striding across the white concrete pavement towards them. Juliet started to wind down the window, but he put up his hand to stop her and quickly opened the door and slid into the seat beside her. It was typical of his thoughtfulness that he did not wish her to spoil the air-conditioned atmosphere of the car, and she gave him a grateful smile.

'I didn't mean to disturb you,' she apologised. 'But Ali always slows down as we drive past the Clinic. You'll have to invite him in one day and show him around.'

'Wouldn't you like to be shown around yourself?'

'I'd love it, but I don't want to bother you.'

'As I'm only here because you agreed to accompany me. . . .'

'I don't believe that,' she smiled.

'It's true,' he said emphatically. 'You're the only woman I could have asked.'

She knew he meant that he was not afraid she would want to keep him tied to her once they left Doria. The knowledge should have gratified her, yet it made her despondent. Surreptitiously she studied him. He looked as if he had all the time in the world. But then he always gave this impression no matter what pressure he was under, and she knew this was the only way he managed to cope with his enormous amount of work. Again she was conscious of the tiredness around his eyes.

'Is the woman I saw getting out of your car the new surgeon?' she asked.

'Yes.' He was alert again, sitting forward with one hand on the car door. 'She says she isn't tired from her flight, so I thought we should ask her to dine with us tonight. It would give me a chance to talk to her and for both of you to get acquainted.'

'I can't see her having much time for me,' Juliet murmured.

'I wish you wouldn't deprecate yourself!' Damon was unusually sharp. 'You may not have any medical knowledge, but you have a lively mind, which you should exercise.'

Before she could recover from this unexpected criticism, he left the car, and she watched him stride back to the Clinic, where she glimpsed the shadowy figure of the woman still waiting for him.

Driving home, Juliet conceded that Damon's comment was justified, though she was surprised he had not made allowance for the blow her self-esteem had suffered at Perry's desertion of her. She had not lacked confidence before she had met Perry, but her delight in being allowed to join his Company had made her excessively pliable. She had wanted to be the sort of girl Perry would love and, as a result, her own personality had disappeared.

It was strange that Damon, who was just as dominant as Perry, though in a far more subtle way, should not like his women to be docile. But he didn't, and while she remained his wife, she owed it to him to be more the way he wanted.

Abruptly she leaned forward and asked Ali to drive her to the shopping centre.

Happily he complied. He liked to be seen at the wheel of the big blue car on whose bonnet fluttered the yellow and black pennant given only to Sheik Quima's household and his closest friends.

'You wish to buy something special, madame?' Ali enquired.

'Not really. I want to look around. Leave me at the

top of the main street and meet me at the bottom end in an hour's time.'

'If Madam wait till I park car, I accompany her.'

Not sure if Damon had instructed him always to do so, she agreed, and shortly afterwards they were strolling down the main street, Ali a few steps behind her. Apart from a newly-built department store it was lined with small shops selling goods of every description, all of them imported. In the main, American goods predominated, since most of the foreigners living here came from the United States, though there was also a fair number of Scandinavians. It was easy to picture these big blond men working in the oilfields, their pale eyes burning with enthusiasm each time another oil well gushed.

There were very few Dorian women to be seen, and those that were wore European dress and had no veils to mask their small, thickish features. Wealthy Dorian women remained within the seclusion of their homes, waited on by servants who did their shopping and cooking, while the poorer ones could not afford to buy in this part of the city. Ali had once taken Juliet to the market on the northern side of the capital, and she had been intrigued by the hundreds of stalls and the black-garbed, veiled women milling around them, only their hands and eyes visible as they picked out fruit and vegetables and haggled over prices.

But the boutiques in modern Kuwan would have done justice to Paris and Rome, and saved Dorian women the trouble of going abroad to buy their clothes. One boutique, slightly larger than the others, caught Juliet's eye and she paused to look in the window. Three blue dresses were skilfully draped on stands, each one in a different shade and style. She knew at once that Perry would have adored them.

Pushing the thought away, she stepped inside the shop, emerging an hour later with enough parcels to satisfy Ali. She had spent considerably more than she had planned, but the saleswoman had been persuasive and her taste had been identical with Juliet's and not at all like Perry's, for which reason Juliet found herself trying on vivid colours instead of muted ones, and dramatic styles instead of the simpler Druid garments he had favoured for her.

Perry. How much she was thinking of him today! Was it because he was thinking of her? She wished she could believe it, but somehow she knew it wasn't true. Out of sight, out of mind was the axiom on which he based his life. Not that he did it in a calculating way. He was merely so concerned with himself and that he could not spare time for anyone who was not part of his world.

As I'm not, Juliet thought, and waited to feel her usual pang of self-pity. None came. Surprised, she continued to walk. Had time already lessened the grief his departure had caused? If this were so, she should be glad. Yet she wasn't, for it showed that her love for him was as fickle as his own had been. Perhaps I'm growing a second skin, she thought. It isn't that I love Perry less, it's just that I'm learning to cope with it better.

The knowledge made her feel more her own woman, and the smile she gave Ali as she climbed into the car was such a happy one that he giggled.

'Is good for Madame to shop. She do so each day, yes?'

'I doubt that. Dr Masters would think I was very extravagant if I did.'

'If Madame happy, the Doctor happy,' Ali replied, taking his place behind the wheel.

Juliet sighed. How wrong Ali was! But then he only saw the surface of her relationship with Damon. For the first time since her marriage she wished there was some truth in what the young Arab had said. Damon was such a wonderful person that he deserved to be happy.

CHAPTER SEVEN

THAT night Juliet wore one of her new dresses. It was
apple green and brought out the russet lights in her
brown hair, as well as doing amazing things for her
eyes. How huge they looked tonight! She darkened
the lids with shadow and applied mascara to her long
lashes. Since her marriage to Damon she rarely wore
any, afraid it made her look too theatrical. But tonight
she did not care. In musical parlance, it was all the
stops out.

Stepping back from the mirror to look at herself full-
length, she saw she had gained weight since leaving
England, and on an impulse decided to weigh herself
on the scales in Damon's bathroom.

She rarely went into his suite, and never when he
was present, and tonight she felt as if she were tres-
passing on a private domain. A navy silk dressing-
gown was draped across a chair and black suede
slippers stood on the carpet beneath. He had not yet
come home and she had to be quick if she wanted to
avoid him.

In the bathroom she slipped off her shoes and stepped on to the scales. She was four pounds heavier than
she had been two months ago. She put on her shoes
and looked at herself in Damon's mirror. The angular
contours of her body had gone and one noticed the
curve of her hips instead of the hip-bones themselves.
The same applied to her shoulders and arms, which
no longer seemed to be bisected sharply by her collar-

bones. But there were still delicate hollows at her throat, and her neck was long and slender. Her breasts were fuller, though, and were well defined by the skilfully cut bodice of her dress.

'You look quite good,' she said to her reflection, and almost jumped out of her skin when a deep voice said: 'I could pay you a better compliment than that.'

Swinging round, she saw Damon emerge from behind the door. 'How long have you been watching me?' she asked.

'Only a moment. It seemed a pity to disturb your self-appraisal.'

'I was wondering if I'd put on too much weight,' she confessed.

'The answer is no. You were too thin when I met you. For my personal taste, you should even put on a few pounds more.'

'Really?' she asked, pleased by this.

'Fat or thin, you're a beautiful woman, Juliet.'

Their gaze held and warmth came into her cheeks. He had changed into his silk dressing gown and she was uncomfortably aware that he had nothing on underneath it.

'I m-must get some scales for my own bathroom,' she stammered, backing to the door.

'I'll have these sent in to you. Actually this room and bath should be yours. In estate agent's terms, it's the master suite.'

'But *you're* the master,' she smiled. 'That's what Ali always calls you.'

'Are you the mistress?' he quipped.

'I'm sure you're far too proper ever to have one!'

His look was quizzical. 'Don't bet on it.'

Smiling, she went to the door.

'Monique will be here in half an hour,' he called. 'I told Cook to hold back dinner for an hour. I'm afraid I got tied up at the Clinic longer than I anticipated.'

'I thought you'd be working less now you have someone to help you.'

'Wait until Monique has settled in,' he smiled. 'Then she'll try to see I have no work at all.'

Juliet was curious to meet the woman who could even begin to think she could do Damon's work.

'I still don't know her second name,' she said as he joined her in the living room a little later.

'Lamont. Her husband was a Professor of psychiatry in Montreal.'

'Was?'

'He died a year ago from a brain haemorrhage. Monique diagnosed it.' He hesitated. 'I flew over to give a second opinion, but it was hopeless. If he'd lived, he would have been a vegetable.'

'I hadn't realised Dr Lamont was a widow.' Juliet looked at him enquiringly. 'If she's a surgeon does one call her Mrs?'

'No. It's only in England that surgeons are called Mr and not Doctor. But Monique's a French-Canadian, so you can safely call her Doctor.' He half smiled. 'If she runs true to form she'll insist you call her by her first name, anyway.'

A car purred into the grounds of the villa and he went into the hall. A soft, feminine voice was heard, then he and a woman came into the living room.

Monique Lamont was considerably younger than Juliet had anticipated. Older than herself, but still only in her early thirties, with the bandbox freshness one associated with women from the North American continent. She had precisely modelled features: a wide, well-shaped mouth, a high forehead from which auburn hair waved back—its colour so natural that it was hard to tell if it was artificial or real—and steady blue eyes above a small nose. She was tall for a woman and the top of her head reached to Damon's chin, which made her a good five feet nine, every inch of it well co-ordinated and shapely.

'So you're Damon's wife?' A firm hand clasped Juliet's. 'I must say I never thought I'd live to see the day. All Damon's friends have long since given up hope that he'd take the plunge.'

'It was head first, too,' Damon grinned. 'Until I put the ring on Juliet's hand I was scared she'd let out the water!'

Monique laughed and gave him an affectionate look. 'Knowing you, I'm sure you made certain her hands were tied. You never leave anything to chance.'

'Be careful what you say,' Damon warned. 'Juliet's still wearing the rose-tinted spectacles of a bride.'

Monique gave Juliet a smile. 'I'm sure you've already discovered that your husband knows exactly what he wants and how to get it.'

Recollecting the suddenness of his proposal and her almost immediate acceptance of it, Juliet nodded. She was saved from answering by Damon, who had gone over to the drinks trolley and was holding aloft a bottle of champagne. Seeing the ice bucket, she guessed he had ordered it to be filled when he had telephoned the cook and told her what to prepare for dinner. She had been surprisingly irritated when she had returned home this afternoon, all set to cajole the cook into making them something extra special, to find that Damon had already done so. Even more irritating, she could not fault his choice of menu. One would have thought that with so much work at the Clinic, he would have no time to concern himself with household trivia. Not that he usually did; today was one of the few occasions when he had, and it was obvious Dr Lamont was important to him.

'You have a lovely home, Damon,' Monique said as she accepted a glass of champagne from him.

'I still prefer my own in London.'

He handed a glass to Juliet and settled himself on the settee beside her. In the normal course of events he never sat close to her, and she knew he only did it now in order to make their visitor believe his marriage was a normal one.

'I hope you'll find your apartment to your liking,' he continued, speaking to Monique. 'If you need anything at any time, let me know. Sheik Quima is anxious to do everything he can to keep us happy.'

'That makes a change from the usual hospital administration,' came the amused reply. 'I must say he's built a magnificent clinic for you. Your getting it from him was a great achievement.'

'So was my getting *you* to come out here.' He gave her a warm smile before turning to Juliet. 'I didn't realise until today that Monique turned down a post at the John Hopkins in order to come out here.'

Juliet looked bewildered and the woman chuckled.

'You aren't impressing your wife, Damon. Quite rightly, she can't see why I should prefer to work at the John Hopkins when I can work with you. Which goes to show that women are far more sensible than men. I can learn more here in three months than I can in a year anywhere else.'

'You exaggerate.'

'I don't. You're untouchable in your field.'

'Luckily that isn't true,' he replied quickly. 'Don't let your admiration for my character give you illusions about my medical ability.'

The woman laughed and Juliet, watching them, felt an outsider. She had not anticipated there would be such ease between Damon and his new colleague. He had said he had known her for years, but until she had seen them together she had not guessed how much they liked each other. Could it be more than liking on Monique Lamont's part? The woman had married someone else and would surely not have done so if she loved Damon. Somehow Juliet could not imagine her wanting a man and not fighting to get him.

'Some more champagne, darling?'

Damon interrupted her thoughts and she shook her head, but watched him as he crossed the room to replenish his visitor's glass. Seen together they made a striking couple, both of them tall and exuding confidence and vitality. Monique Lamont is far more suitable for Damon than I am, Juliet thought, and wondered if he was thinking this too. They were too far away for her to hear their entire conversation, but a few words drifted over to her: medical terms which she did not understand. After several minutes she became impatient. Had Damon completely forgotten that his wife was in the room?

'You shouldn't talk shop to your guest,' she said in a teasing voice. 'You're a very bad host, Damon.'

'Monique isn't an ordinary guest,' he replied. 'She's one of my closest friends.' His well-shaped hand rested momentarily on Monique's arm. 'I really am delighted to have you working here.'

For an instant the man and woman looked into each other's eyes and Juliet felt that neither of them was aware of her presence. Her temper began to rise and with an effort she controlled it.

'I suppose you heard that Jack Holmes has the chair in Gynaecology in Adelaide?' Monique said to Damon.

'Yes, I did. But what about his wife? She was a talented sculptor, as I remember.'

'She left Jack and went to live in an artists' commune in Perugia.'

'That must have been a shock for him,' Damon replied. 'He considered himself God's gift to woman.'

'God's gift—period,' Monique said firmly.

Damon chuckled and Juliet cut across it by saying dinner was ready.

Over the meal, conversation became more general and Juliet was able to join in the conversation. Monique was curious about life in Doria and seemed to believe that Juliet lived a coffee-in-the-morning and cocktails-in-the-afternoon existence. Juliet was tempted to say that she too had had a successful career, but the knowledge that this was in the past tempered her anger and she was able to respond to Monique's questions calmly.

After dinner Damon went to take a telephone call in his study, leaving the two women alone.

'Damon worked like a Trojan to try to save my husband's life,' Monique said unexpectedly. 'Even when other doctors said it was hopeless, he refused to give up.'

'It must have been a terrible blow for you when your husband died,' Juliet said sympathetically.

'I lost one of the best friends I had.' The woman looked down at her hands which lay folded in her lap. They were square, capable ones, with nails cut short and devoid of colour, the fingers ringless except for a narrow gold band. 'I was never in love with Ted. He proposed to me one particularly miserable Christmas, and in a fit of weakness I said yes.'

'You speak as if you regret it.'

'I regret that I didn't love him. In the last year of his life, when I knew he was dying, I pretended I did.' She sighed. 'I liked to think I fooled him.'

'Fooled whom?' Damon asked, coming into the room.

'I was talking about Ted,' Monique said quietly.

'He was very happy with you.' Damon's voice was gruff and for the second time that evening he placed his hand on Monique's arm. 'You shouldn't look back, my dear. You have too many years ahead of you.'

'I'm thirty-five. Not so young.'

'How's that supposed to make *me* feel?'

'It's different for men.' The patrician nose wrinkled at him. 'If I want to have a family I have to start soon.' The blue eyes twinkled at Juliet. 'I hope I'm not being tactless?'

Juliet smiled, but for the life of her could not think of a witty response. Though men did not have the same age barrier as women when it came to fathering children, she knew that most of them wanted a family while they were still young enough to share their pleasures with them. She wondered if Damon felt the same. If he did, he too was leaving it rather late.

She watched him settle into a chair. The lamp shining behind Monique Lamont also shone upon him, enclosing them both in the same radiance. It made her see them as more than a medical partnership, and she was convinced that the woman was in love with him. Yet in marrying another man she had accepted the fact that Damon did not love her. Juliet ran her tongue over her lips. If this were so, had Monique come to Doria in the hope that now she was here again, he would see her differently?

'Were you surprised when you heard Damon was married?' Juliet asked abruptly.

For an infinitesimal moment Monique was motionless. 'Very,' she said. 'I only learned of it when I got here.' Blue eyes glinted at Damon. 'Why didn't you tell me when you offered me the job? You kept your letter as formal as if you didn't even know me.'

'I wanted you to consider the position on the merit of the work alone.'

'You could still have told me about your wife. I feel embarrassed at not having brought you a wedding present.'

'Thank heavens you didn't!' He looked alarmed. 'We already have a whole stack of them waiting for us when we get back to England. According to Mother's last letter there are five silver toast racks, a dozen coffee services and countless silver ink stands, desk clocks and barometers.'

'You never told me that before!' Juliet was astonished.

'And get you excited for nothing?' he smiled.

Juliet was flummoxed. She did not believe Damon's reason for his reticence, yet could think of no other.

'Jet lag is catching up on me,' said Monique, rising. 'That, and your excellent wine.'

'I'll drive you home.' Damon rose too. 'Tomorrow you should be getting your own car and driver.'

'What luxury!' Monique came across to Juliet. 'It was kind of you to invite me over at such short notice. When I'm settled in my own place and have inspected the food market, I hope you'll come to dinner.'

'That's not as ominous as it sounds,' Damon chuckled, draping a cobwebby shawl over the woman's shoulders. 'Monique's a fantastic cook and always produces something highly spicy and intriguing.'

'I'd rather that was a character reference than a description of my culinary abilities,' the woman laughed, and extended her hand to Juliet.

When they had gone, Juliet prowled the living-room, too restless to go to bed. Through the windows she saw the dark garden. A few lamps illuminated the palm trees that skirted the perimeter of the grounds, but beyond this there was nothing but blackness and a few pinpoints of stars in the canopy of blue velvet that formed the sky.

The servants had their own quarters at the far end of the garden, but Ali was still in the house, for he had strict instructions never to retire at night until Damon was home. She wondered where Monique was living. Most of the European staff at the Clinic lived within walking distance of each other, but Damon himself had refused to consider it.

'When I leave the Clinic I like to put it completely behind me,' he had said. 'If we were staying here longer than a year, I'd get a weekend place somewhere else.'

'Do you have one in England?' Juliet had asked.

'Yes. A small cottage near my parents. It means that if I don't want to take Jenkins down with me I can always drop in to my mother's for a meal.'

She had been amused. 'You're so interested in food, yet you eat sparingly. Is that how you manage to stay so lean?'

'Lean? I weigh considerably more than you.'

'At six feet three, so you should.'

'No one's ever called me lean,' he repeated.

'You have well-formed bones,' she added, 'but there isn't much fat on them.'

'You sound like a butcher inspecting a joint!'

She had laughed again and, remembering this now, realised it had been one of the few occasions when she had felt close to him. Tonight she had felt the exact opposite. Seeing him with his attention focused on another woman had made her feel strangely alone.

Another twenty minutes went by and still he did not return. Even if Monique Lamont lived on the other side of Kuwan he should have been back by now. He must have gone into her apartment for a nightcap. Deciding it was ridiculous to wait for him like an anxious wife, Juliet went to her room. As long as Ali was in the house it didn't matter to her what time Damon came home. He could stay out all night as far as she was concerned.

She was in bed trying to read when she heard him come in. His steps were quiet as he walked along the corridor, and she heard him pause as he saw the light shining from under her door.

'May I come in for a moment, Juliet?'

'Of course.' She glanced down to make sure she was suitably covered by her nightdress and hitched the thin sheet higher over her breasts.

Damon came across the room and paused at the foot of her bed. The last time he had stood in such a position he had told her he could do nothing to cure her illness. She had never thought then that she would end up marrying him.

'I'm sorry I was so long,' he apologised. 'Monique and I started talking again about old times.'

'They must have been very long old times.' Juliet

saw him give her a sharp look and said quickly: 'She's nice. Younger than I expected, though.'

'But already in the top flight in her field.'

'It's a pity she hasn't remarried.'

He was amused. 'You sound like one of my sisters! They're born matchmakers. But Monique is happy as she is.'

'How do you know?'

'Through years of association.' He slipped one hand into the pocket of his jacket, another of his gestures which always made him look withdrawn and aloof.

'Then I suppose you know she didn't love her husband?' Juliet said. 'She married him because she was lonely.'

Silence met this comment and Juliet wished she had not spoken.

'Do you know her well enough to make such a statement?' he asked.

'She told me herself. You came in on the tail end of that conversation, if you remember. Personally, I think she'd have preferred to marry *you*.'

His brows met above his nose. They were delicately arched brows, a shade darker than his hair. 'Monique is a trusted and respected colleague. To see her in any other way would be an embarrassment for us both. It's a pity you didn't keep your own counsel.'

'I didn't know you liked to bury your head in the sand.'

This time he did not disguise the sharpness of his look. 'What's the matter, Juliet? You aren't usually spiteful.'

She lowered her eyes. 'I'm sorry, Damon. It was wrong of me to repeat what Monique said. But I couldn't help thinking you'd have had a much better deal if you'd married Monique, instead of me.'

Once again there was silence and it went on for so long that she was not sure if he intended to reply.

'If Monique does happen to be fond of me,' he said finally, 'then asking her to become my wife would have been unspeakably cruel.'

'You might have fallen in love with her. Propinquity does strange things.'

'Propinquity has already had its chance. We worked closely together when she was studying in London.' His expression was ironic. 'Perhaps propinquity will affect *our* relationship.'

Colour flooded Juliet's face. 'Be serious, Damon!'

'What makes you think I'm not? We get on very well and you've shown yourself to be an amusing and understanding companion. You even ignore my bad temper when I'm overtired.'

'Any woman would do the same.'

'But not any woman is as beautiful as you.'

She was pleased but tried not to show it. 'I didn't think you noticed what I looked like.'

'I notice everything about you.'

She tilted her head, unaware of the light flooding on to her shoulders and making the curve of her breasts visible through the fine cover of the sheet.

'I suppose it's because you're a doctor,' she said.

'I'm a man too.' His voice was deeper. 'You looked exceptionally lovely tonight. Green is an excellent foil for your hair. I'd also like to see you in red.'

Juliet was so surprised that she lost the embarrassment that had invaded her at his compliment. 'I never imagined you would like such a vivid colour,' she said.

'Normally I don't. But it would suit you.'

'Do you see me as a scarlet woman?' she asked humorously.

'You could never be that. You look too innocent.'

'I *am* innocent.'

'I rather thought you were.'

The way his eyes moved over her body told her what was in his mind and she was once again filled with embarrassment. She tried to overcome it by reminding herself that Damon was a doctor, and that as a doctor he had examined her body. But the thought of him touching her today was quite different, and she shied away from it.

'We should entertain more,' she blurted out, saying the first thing that came into her head. 'I'm beginning to find the long days boring, and if I had some parties to plan. . . .'

'By all means. I was actually giving you a chance to get used to your wobbly pins before suggesting it myself.'

His non-medical way of describing her illness made her laugh, and he knew immediately why.

'Humour is often the best way of overcoming one's fear,' he said gently. 'And now that you're ready to face life again, I'll make out a list of the people I'd like us to invite over. But don't overtax yourself.'

Juliet lay wakeful for a long time after Damon had gone, unexpectedly excited by the prospect of entertaining in her own home. What a good thing she had suggested it to Damon! After all, she was his wife and likely to remain so for at least another year; it was a pity to waste that year when she could be enjoying it with the well-mannered and intelligent man whose name she bore.

Having come to this conclusion she felt much more at peace with herself. She also felt she had put Monique into her rightful place as Damon's colleague, and nothing more. It was a satisfying thought, and she turned off the light and closed her eyes.

CHAPTER EIGHT

THE following evening, as proof that he remembered his conversation with her, Damon gave Juliet a typewritten list of everyone they should entertain.

'But I don't want you to overtire yourself,' he warned again.

'You keep telling me I'm not an invalid,' she remonstrated, 'so don't treat me as one.'

'Point taken. In future I'll regard you as a normal, full-blooded young woman.'

She looked at him suspiciously, but his expression was bland, and she knew he had not made the remark with any specific purpose in mind. The trouble was that she had become so conscious of him that it made her read hidden meanings into his every comment. It was as well to remember that Damon was not the type to make ambiguous statements; he said what he meant, and meant what he said.

A faint sigh escaped her. If only she were as self-sufficient! She was learning from him, though, and would never again let anyone organise her life the way Perry had done. Only by remaining true to herself would she be able to establish a genuine relationship with a man.

An image of Lilah came into her mind: the heavily made-up face, the voluptuous figure and flamboyant clothes. Yet Perry had always disliked too much make-up, vivid colours and obvious sexuality, which only went to reinforce her decision.

'Why the pensive look?' Damon questioned. 'Or are your thoughts secret?'

'I don't have any secrets from you.'

'I was taught never to believe a woman when she said that.'

She laughed. It was nice when his serious façade cracked to show the humorous man behind it.

'How is Monique settling down at the Clinic?' she asked.

'Excellently. She's already begun to help me with the new patients. But don't let's talk about my work. When I come home I like to forget it.'

Juliet was put out. Although she understood the reason for Damon's attitude, if he never discussed his work with her he would be excluding her from a major part of his life. But then why shouldn't he? Their marriage was a pretence and he had made no commitment to share anything with her except his name.

'I think we'll give our first dinner party on Saturday,' she said. 'That will give me a week to plan it.'

'And to buy yourself a new dress.'

'What makes you think I will?'

'Won't you?' His mouth curved upwards. 'The caterpillar is becoming a butterfly.'

'What a compliment!' she scoffed. 'I thought I was already a butterfly.'

'You were—and I apologise for my heavy-handedness. Let's say you were a Meadow Brown and that you're now becoming a Swallowtail.'

She laughed again, but remembered the comment when she went shopping the following day. This time she visited several boutiques and was astonished by the high prices of the clothes. But then this was a country of enormous wealth, where the rich had too much of everything and the poor had nothing.

She said as much to Damon when she saw him at lunchtime, and his reply surprised her.

'The situation won't last much longer. There's growing unrest among the masses and it only needs a spark to ignite it.'

'A spark from within?'

'It's more likely to come from outside. Doria has some envious neighbours who'd like to get their hands on its oilfields.'

'Do you think there might be a war here?' she asked.

'Personally, I do, though the Sheik believes he can stave it off. But let's talk of happier things.'

'Why? I'm not an imbecile, you know. It's only my legs that are weak, not my brain.'

'My *dear*!' Damon was unusually disconcerted. 'That's the second stupid thing I've said to you in a matter of days. I do apologise.'

'You needn't. You're usually the kindest, most understanding of men.'

Pinkness tinged his skin. It made his eyes look greener and Juliet realised how handsome he was. Dear Damon. He deserved every happiness and it was awful to think she did not love him. The thought startled her. Damon did not want her to love him and he would be embarrassed if she did.

'I won't be home to dinner tonight.' He said into the silence. 'I'm having it with Monique. I was hoping I could explain the Clinic routine to her during our normal working hours, but it's impossible. No one seems capable of doing anything without consulting me first, and I don't get a moment to call my own. At least in the evening I can look forward to a few clear hours.'

'Why not invite her here again?'

'It would mean leaving you immediately afterwards. I thought it better if we didn't attempt any socialising but got straight down to work.' His eyes narrowed. 'You don't mind, do you?'

Surprisingly Juliet did, but she had no intention of admitting it. 'Why should I? I'll use the time to go through the cupboards and sort out the linen and cutlery.'

'Don't buy anything. The Sheik has offered to give us all we need and he would consider it a slight if we didn't accept.' Damon glanced at his watch and rose. 'Don't wait up for me tonight. I'll probably be late.'

Juliet spent the rest of the day checking through the household items. She also made a list of the food required for the dinner party. As Damon was not in for a meal she gave the cook the evening off, assuring him she could easily make herself a snack. It was a good idea to do some domestic chores. Nine months from now and she would have to do everything for herself. The idea of returning to a small flat in London, perhaps only a bedsitter, was a dismal prospect, but it was unwise not to think of it.

Soon after eight o'clock she went into the kitchen to make a toasted cheese sandwich and a cup of coffee. Ali was ironing in the small room beyond it, and she glimpsed one of Damon's jackets. It brought him so vividly to mind that she swung round, almost expecting him to be behind her. But the kitchen was empty and she busied herself making some toast and the coffee. She set a place at the corner of the kitchen table, unwilling to eat in solitary splendour in the dining area. As the percolator bubbled she put cheese slices on the toast and slipped it under the grill. It bubbled and turned brown and she set it on to a plate. Holding the plate in one hand and the percolator in the other, she turned towards the table.

The loss of strength in her legs took her by surprise, and before she could save herself she fell to the floor, narrowly missing hitting her head on the edge of the table. The toast and cheese slithered across the tiles and the percolator crashed to the ground beside her. The lid shot off and scalding liquid splashed over her leg.

Juliet gave a scream of pain and Ali rushed in. He stared down at her with frightened black eyes.

'Madame fainted?'

She shook her head, in too much pain to speak, and pointed to her leg. Ali immediately lifted the percolator and carried it over to the sink, then came back with a towel with which he wiped the boiling coffee from the floor.

'Shall I carry Madame into the living room?' he asked anxiously.

Reluctant for him to lift her, Juliet shook her head. The first agonising pain had abated and movement had returned to her legs. Carefully she rose, but was quick to sit down again on a kitchen chair. The skin from her knee down to mid-calf was one scarlet blotch and burned as though it were on fire. Unfortunately she had no milk to put on it, for only the tinned or dried kind was available here.

Shakily she told Ali to bring her a towel soaked in cold water, and she wrapped it round her scalded leg.

'Do we have a first-aid kit here?' she asked.

'I not know. You want I call the master?'

'No. There's no point worrying him for nothing.'

'Madame's accident not nothing. The master angry if I not let him know.'

'He won't be angry with you, Ali. I'll take the responsibility.'

Still holding the sopping towel to her leg, Juliet hobbled to her bedroom. The pain made her feel nauseous, and she was angry that Damon did not have the foresight to keep a first aid box in the house.

Tears filled her eyes. Why had fate been so cruel to her? It had not only taken away her health and her ability to earn a living in her chosen career, but the man she had hoped to marry. Shakily she took off her dress and lay on the bed. She unwound the towel and saw that the skin below her knee was an angry scarlet. If she had been able to call a doctor without Damon knowing, she would have done so.

Somewhere near at hand a car door slammed. She was not expecting any visitors and it was too early for Damon to be returning. Then she heard him call her name, but before she could answer she heard Ali speak and knew that the young man was regaling him with news of her accident.

The next instant the door of her bedroom burst open and Damon strode in. Without a word he whipped back the sheet and stared at her leg. It was not a pretty sight and she averted her eyes from it, focusing them on Damon instead. His lips were clamped so tightly together that their normal well-shaped curve was a straight line. Still without a word he went out, and she remained where she was, her heart thumping as heavily as if she were guilty of some crime. Then he was back again with a large box. From it he took gauze and a tube of cream, and with deft movements let the cream ooze over her burning skin. It felt cool and then numbing, and as the pain ebbed, some of her normal spirit returned.

'If I'd known where you kept the first aid box, I could have prevented my skin from blistering.'

'You'd do better to prevent any further unnecessary accidents.' His voice was harsher than she had ever heard it. 'I thought you'd made out a list of the things you shouldn't do?'

'I did. But I forgot them.'

'Then I'd better engage a companion to remind you.'

'Don't be silly!' She saw his lips tighten again and made an apologetic gesture. 'I'm sorry, Damon, but you're fussing for nothing.'

'I'd hardly call a scalded leg nothing. Don't you know what a shock it is to the nervous system?'

'I'm not a bit shocked. I'm fine.'

But she wasn't, and her violent trembling gave her away.

'I'll get you something to drink,' he said, and went out again.

He left the door open so that he could hear if she called, but nothing would have induced her to do so, although her trembling had increased and there was a heavy constriction in her throat by the time he came back with a brandy.

'I've asked Ali to make you a cup of tea, but meanwhile, drink this.'

She took it and sipped, then leaned back and closed her eyes. She was aware of Damon beside her but he did not speak, and nor did she. By the time Ali arrived with her tea, her trembling had ceased and she was feeling better.

Damon poured her a cup and then sat on the edge of

the bed, careful not to move the mattress in case it hurt her leg.

'I hope you won't give me another fright like that,' he said in measured tones. 'Your legs can give way at any time and you should always keep one hand free. Remember that.'

'I *do* try.'

'Trying isn't good enough, Juliet. You *must* remember.'

'You're right, Damon. It was silly of me. I mean, you don't want to be landed with a total invalid, do you—even if it's only for a year.'

'It's not *my* well-being I'm concerned with, it's yours.'

He rested against the foot rest at the end of the bed and undid his jacket. It fell open and she saw his brown silk tie and an expanse of cream silk shirt. He leaned one arm behind him and the material pulled. A button fell off and she saw a patch of silky skin.

'Damn!' he muttered, and retrieved it from the folds of the sheet.

'Give me the button and I'll sew it on for you,' she smiled.

'Ali can do it.'

'Let me. I feel so useless, Damon, that if I can do any little thing to help you....'

'You've made it possible for me to come to Doria. That's more than enough.'

'You always say that,' she protested.

'Only when you say you feel useless.'

He smiled back at her and she marvelled that he should still be so grateful, when he had done far more for her. In that sense he was unlike Perry, who lapped up appreciation like a child lapped up icecream. But no one could call Damon a child; he was a man in every sense of the word.

'You should have a proper wife,' she blurted out.

'Are you offering yourself?'

Her eyes flew to his. He was unsmiling, but she refused to believe he was serious and made an effort to appear composed.

'I mean it, Damon. You have so much to offer a woman. And you'd make a super father.'

'But not *your* father figure, I hope?' he enquired dryly.

'Oh no. You're far too young and handsome for that.'

He laughed. It put wrinkles around his eyes yet he looked suddenly younger and happier. It was hard for her to realise how important a man he was, and again she was astonished that she had had the luck to become part of his life.

'You should definitely get married,' she reiterated. 'All work and no play, and you'll end up with a thrombosis.'

'One doesn't need to be married in order to play,' he commented humorously.

Head on one side, she studied him. 'I can't see you with a girl-friend. You're not the type.'

'That's true,' he agreed, eyes gleaming. 'If I had a girl-friend, I'm not the type to let anyone see me.'

'You're not taking me seriously, Damon,' she pouted. 'Because I think it's the brandy talking, not you.'

She giggled, deciding this could well be the reason why she felt so at ease with this big, gentle man.

'I'll get you a sleeping pill,' he said prosaically. 'It will ensure you get a good night's rest.'

Because her leg was still throbbing Juliet did not object. She swallowed the pill he brought her and lay

down. It was only then that she realised the sheet was
not covering her, and was glad her nightdress was
cotton and not voile silk. But it still showed the contours of her body and she reminded herself quickly
that Damon was a doctor and used to seeing women in
all stages of undress. It was a reassuring thought in
one way, yet not in another.

'Call me if you need me during the night,' he said.
'I'll leave your door open and mine as well.' He rested
his hand on her shoulder. His fingers were gentle and
he stroked them along the curve of her neck.

He was at the door when she called him. 'Why did
you come back so early, Damon?'

'I didn't like the idea of leaving you here by yourself.'

He went out before she could comment and she
closed her eyes and hoped the pill would soon take
effect. Kind Damon. He deserved more than she could
give him.

For the next few days Damon insisted that Juliet
keep all pressure off her injured leg. The ointment he
had put on it prevented it from blistering badly,
though it was still inflamed. However, she was determined not to cancel the dinner party and went ahead
with the arrangements.

More than ever she appreciated the excellent staff
Sheik Quima had provided for them. Both Ali and the
cook and maid had worked with Europeans before and
did not need to be taught Western customs. They were
honest and hard-working and were genuinely concerned when they learned of her mishap.

News of it travelled fast. She was sure Damon had
not gossiped at the Clinic and assumed that her servants had talked to other servants who had passed on

the news to their employers. Within a few days flowers, chocolates and get-well cards arrived from people she barely knew, and some she did not know at all. Diligently she wrote thank-you notes and put their names on a list of people to be invited to future parties.

On the Friday, Sheik Quima arrived without warning. Damon was at the Clinic and Juliet was aghast at the prospect of entertaining such an illustrious guest on her own. But he turned out to be extremely easy—despite his hawk-like appearance—and spoke excellent English.

'Your husband came to see me this morning,' he explained when he had settled himself and accepted the glass of coffee and sweetmeats which Ali, knowing the protocol, had served them. 'He informed me of your accident and I wished to see for myself that all was well with you.'

She assured him she was much better and then complimented him on the Clinic he had built.

'I only provided the money,' he said, with a lift of white-garbed shoulders. 'Your husband has contributed far more. It was no easy decision for him to leave his London hospital and spend a year out here. At first he refused, as you know, and I did not try to persuade him otherwise. When he cabled me and said he was willing to come after all, I knew it was the will of Allah.'

Sheik Quima went on talking and Juliet made the right replies, but her mind was busy analysing what she had just learned. Why had Damon changed his mind about coming here? Was it because he had not considered the possibility of marriage until he had met her? Or had he *wanted* to marry her and manufactured a reason for getting her to accept his proposal?

This latter idea was so preposterous that she dismissed it. Yet it remained in the back of her mind, and she was glad when the Sheik finally left and she could give free rein to her thoughts.

She was no nearer a conclusion when Damon returned home and, unexpectedly self-conscious with him, she watched him more carefully than usual. What an inscrutable man he was! It was impossible to know what went on in his mind. With Perry it had been different. He had always been so open. She frowned. Perry had only appeared open. Had he actually been so, his behaviour would not have come as such a shock to her.

'Sheik Quima came to see me,' she said aloud.

'So I gather. You should consider yourself honoured.' Damon nodded towards her leg. 'How does it feel today?'

'Much better. Though it still looks like a sausage.'

'Looks aren't important. It's what a person is that matters.'

'Do you know what I am, Damon?'

'An actress with rare talent.'

He half-turned away from her. 'What else did Sheik Quima have to say for himself?'

'He was full of compliments about you.' She hesitated, then plunged on: 'He said that initially you refused to come here and work. He saw your change of mind as the will of Allah.'

'That's as good a way of seeing it as any other.'

'I wondered if—if it was because ... if you'd changed your mind because....' With all the will in the world she could not continue. Nor could she look at him as she waited for his answer.

'I came here because I considered it my duty,' Damon said quietly. 'I didn't agree to do so in order to give myself a reason for coming to the rescue of a sick young actress.'

'How did you know I thought that?' she demanded.

'You can be very transparent, Juliet.'

'And *you* can be needlessly sarcastic.'

'Because your constant gratitude irritates me?'

'What do you want me to be, then? Ungrateful?'

'No.'

There was a lengthy silence, broken finally by Damon.

'A few days ago you said I was the kindest man you knew. Now you find me sarcastic. Which opinion do you want to stand by?'

'I don't know,' she said wryly. 'I'm afraid to trust my judgment. Look how wrong I was over Perry.'

'We all make mistakes. The main thing is to over-come them. You can't go on living in limbo, you know.'

Seeing his remark as a warning that when they returned to England she would be forced to face the future alone, she said sharply: 'You needn't be afraid that I'll cling to you once we leave Doria.'

'Such a thought never occurred to me.'

'Hasn't it?'

Damon sighed, and when he spoke, it was to change the subject. 'You've been cooped up in the house too long. It's making you introspective. It might be an idea for Ali to take you for a drive each day.'

'Or I could get myself a wheelchair. Then I wouldn't need to bother anyone.'

'You're being childish.'

He put a hand to his mouth to stifle a yawn, and

Juliet's concern for her own tortured emotions vanished as she saw how tired he looked.

'What a thoughtless pig I am!' she exclaimed. 'You've been working six days out of seven for the past three months, and all I do is to pick quarrels with you. Why don't you take a holiday, Damon?'

'Compared with the work I did in London, this *is* a holiday.'

'You don't look very rested. I thought Monique was supposed to ease your workload?'

'Only as far as administration goes. She's a surgeon, not a physician. I still have to see all the patients.'

'Can't you get another doctor like yourself?'

'I thought I was unique.'

His teasing warmed her, making her believe their relationship might be strengthening.

'I can't help worrying about you,' she murmured.

'Don't. I work long hours from choice. I enjoy it.'

Juliet was flummoxed. Was Damon trying to say he did not enjoy being with her? Yet the night he had dined with Monique he had come back early because he had been worried about leaving her alone. She bit back a sigh. Damon was right when he said she was becoming too introspective. Basically she was gregarious, and though her illness had changed this, her natural desire for company was returning. If she continued to remain alone, her irritation would grow and she would use him as a whipping boy.

'I won't nag you any more,' she said firmly. 'If I do, I give you permission to beat me.'

'In anger or in love?'

She laughed. 'Only in anger. I don't see you doing it as a sign of love. You're definitely not the kinky type.'

She went over to him and on an impulse slipped her

arm through his. His body tensed and though he did not draw back, she had a feeling that her proximity worried him. Quickly she took her hand away and went out, not looking back at him in case he saw the hurt in her eyes.

CHAPTER NINE

THE dinner party went with a swing. Juliet's long dress hid her bandaged leg, but the fact that she was wearing one constantly reminded her not to move far away from a chair lest she fall.

There were twelve guests—not too many to spoil the intimacy of the occasion but enough to make conversation easy. Until now she had not seen Damon at a party and was surprised by his conviviality as he dispensed drinks and, later at the table, kept the conversation ranging over a variety of subjects, none of them medical.

Monique had been paired off with Kuwan's most eligible bachelor—a rangy Texan oil tycoon. He seemed smitten with Monique's vibrant good looks but found it hard to believe she was a sufficiently good surgeon to be working with his host, and even more surprised when he discovered she had once turned down the position of neuro-surgeon at the hospital in his home town.

'Maybe you'll consider accepting it when you're through here,' he commented, his voice coming clearly to Juliet during a lull in the conversation.

Juliet was unable to hear Monique's reply, though she noticed the way the woman's eyes turned to Damon as she answered. Juliet was convinced the woman was in love with him, and was sure Damon knew it; that was why his expression always softened when he spoke of her. He never looks at me that way, Juliet thought.

Not even tonight when he saw my new dress. I could appear in three red feathers for all the impact I make on him.

She smoothed the folds of scarlet silk which cascaded to the ground from a tightly nipped-in waist, and gained comfort from the admiring look of one of her guests, a young man who had recently arrived in Kuwan from London to open a branch of a merchant bank. Seeing her eyes on him, he came across to her.

'An excellent dinner, Mrs Masters. The best meal I've had since I arrived here.'

'Food is never good in the hotels,' she agreed. 'I suppose you'll be looking for your own place if you're going to stay here long?'

He nodded and talked at length about the problems he had encountered in setting up his bank. Juliet listened halfheartedly, her main attention focused on Monique, who was recounting some amusing incident that had happened to her. There was no doubt the woman had a powerful personality, but not so strong that it detracted from her feminine qualities. Tonight these were enhanced by a mid-calf dress in floating black organza, caught here and there with tiny silver beads. She looked a bit like a night sky, dark and mysterious, yet with an occasional glimmer of light.

We'd make a great foil for each other, Juliet mused and thought of this again when, a little later, Monique glided over to join her.

'What a lovely party, Juliet. You've obviously got the gift of mixing the right people.'

'Have I?' Juliet asked doubtfully, thinking of the parties she and Perry had given in her apartment in London: lighthearted affairs, noisy with laughter, music, inexpensive food and rough red wine.

'How do you occupy your time here?' Monique asked, bringing Juliet back to the present. 'Do you have many friends?'

'None at all. I find it. . . .' Juliet paused, not sure if Damon had told Monique about her illness.

'I suppose you're worried in case your legs give way at the wrong moment.' Monique's statement showed that he had. 'But you'd be surprised how quickly you'd stop being embarrassed by it.'

'I doubt that.'

'It's true. Take my word for it and give it a try. Go to the European club one afternoon. They have an excellent pool, and if your legs give out on you while you're swimming, you can always float.'

'I'm not much of a swimmer,' Juliet said wryly. 'I'm not much good at anything except acting.'

'Damon says you're a very talented one. Did you play in the West End?'

'Yes. I was a member of Perry Langdon's company at the Carlton.'

'Then you *are* good. He was a boy wonder when I was working in London.'

'Of course, I'd forgotten you were a student there.'

'Hardly a student,' Monique smiled. 'I did a post-graduate course in London.'

'But Damon. . . .'

Monique laughed outright. 'Your husband considers everyone below the level of professor to be a student.'

'Surely not!'

'I'm exaggerating,' Monique admitted. 'Damon treats everyone with respect, no matter what their qualifications. Sometimes I tell him he's too perfect.'

'But perfect to live with,' said Juliet, wishing, for reasons she was reluctant to determine, to make clear to Monique her own position with him.

'I'm sure he'd do anything for *you*,' the woman agreed. 'You're very beautiful, Juliet. Beside you, I feel like a hag.'

Only a confident woman would make such an assertion, and Juliet wondered if Damon had told Monique the real state of his marriage. Shying away from the question, she asked a totally different one.

'Are you pleased you came out here to work?'

'Very much so. It's harder than I thought it would be—emotionally, I mean.'

Juliet's startled eyes met the blue ones, and saw resignation there as well as sadness.

'I love Damon,' Monique said softly. 'But you knew that as soon as you saw us together, didn't you?'

'I suspected it.'

'You have nothing to fear from me. Damon's never seen me as anything more than a friend.'

'Men can be very blind.'

'So can women. He's a great man, Juliet, not only as a doctor but as a person. I hope you appreciate him.'

Juliet nodded, stifling the guilt which these words aroused. She did appreciate Damon, even though she was increasingly irritated by his unruffled calm towards her. Yet were he to behave differently, she would be afraid. I'm becoming too damned introspective, she decided, and knew she should take Monique's advice and go out more.

'Is there a dramatic society in Kuwan?' she demanded of the room.

A startled silence met her question, then everyone spoke at once. There was a music society and a photographic one, but the nearest one could get to drama was the monthly meeting of the poetry club.

'Then I'll start a dramatic society of my own,' Juliet announced. 'With so many foreign nationalities here, we should be able to do some marvellous plays.'

'You'll have half the Clinic staff wanting to join,' Damon told her.

He was standing by the window, partially framed by the gauzy white curtains. The background made him look taller and darker and very much the father figure he had once accused Juliet of thinking him. But he was her husband. Not a real one, it was true, but her husband nonetheless. She felt Monique stir beside her and knew that if the French-Canadian were his wife, he would not be sleeping alone. But then Monique loved him, and would have done anything to arouse a response from him.

Juliet looked at Damon again and saw he was still watching her. Did he never feel the need for a real marriage: the urge to hold a woman in his arms and make love to her? He was a normal man and must surely experience some desire. Work could not prevent this, though it could frequently act as compensation. Yet why should an attractive man like Damon need compensation? He should have married for love.

'Where shall the society meet?' The question, coming from the young banker, brought back Juliet's wandering attention. 'Shall we hire a suite at one of the hotels?'

'That would be too expensive,' another woman replied. 'Isn't there a church hall we could rent?'

'In Kuwan?' Damon chuckled. 'You'd find it easier to hire a tent!'

'I'm quite happy for my house to be used,' the Texan interposed. 'My living room holds forty people, and I doubt if we'll get more than that.'

Everyone began to chip in with suggestions and it was well after one o'clock before the party broke up. Monique was the last to leave, with the Texan hovering in the background anxious to take her home. But at last the house was quiet and Juliet wandered into the living room to make sure no one had left anything behind.

'You can congratulate yourself on a very successful party,' Damon said behind her.

'We can congratulate each other. You were a most attentive host.'

'It was an effort in the last hour. I kept longing for my bed.'

She was instantly contrite. 'Why didn't you give me a signal?'

'You were enjoying yourself too much.'

'Dear Damon!' She touched her hand to his and he caught hold of her fingers and squeezed them tightly before letting go.

'Don't bother clearing up,' he said as she bent to one of the ash-trays. 'The servants have little enough to do as it is.'

She nodded and followed him out. They climbed the stairs together. She was careful to keep one hand firmly on the banister, remembering his warning that she might suddenly fall. Her skirt rustled about her and she lifted the front of it.

'It's a lovely dress,' he commented. 'I'm glad you took my advice and chose red.'

'I didn't think you'd remembered. You made no comment on it when I came down earlier this evening.'

'I didn't want to embarrass you.'

'No woman is embarrassed by a compliment.'

'When I've complimented you before you looked as if you wanted to bite me.'

She laughed, and lowered the hem of her dress as they reached the top of the stairs. They were rarely so close together and his nearness brought a tingle to her body which she tried to stifle. This was Damon, the world-renowned physician who, but for her illness, would never have become part of her life. The doctor and the actress. The phrase made her smile and she turned to tell him. Almost simultaneously her legs buckled, and with amazing speed he caught her round the waist.

'I'm sorry,' she gasped.

'You obviously want to be picked up and carried to bed,' he teased, and swinging her into his arms, did exactly that.

As she was lifted, Juliet put an arm around his neck for support. She felt the tension of his muscles and wished there was some way she could help him to relax. They reached her bedroom and Damon placed her on the bed and went to straighten. Inadvertently her fingers touched his ear and he gave a muffled exclamation and pulled her back into his arms.

'Juliet,' he groaned, and placed his lips on hers.

Instantly she responded, feeling no sense of strangeness in the touch of his mouth.

His hands moved over her, cupping the soft breasts and then travelling across her faintly rounded stomach to the firmer lines of her hips. His mouth lost its gentleness and gave way to something more demanding. The pressure grew in intensity, and she gasped and pulled him down until he was half-lying across her as she lay back on the pillows. Her hair was splayed around her and he twined a strand through his fingers, then rained a storm of kisses upon her face, murmuring soft words which she could not distinguish.

His body was heavy upon her and was racked with deep shudders that told her exactly how much her closeness was affecting him, and what strong control he was keeping on himself. His skin was damp and the heat that emanated from him vibrated on her body, sending out arrows of desire that his gently moving hands heightened to exquisite agony.

She returned kiss for kiss, each one more exploring than the one before; each one increasing rather than diminishing their need. Only the ultimate of giving and taking could do that.

Her hips arched upwards, pressing against the lower part of his body, and he gave another groan. It was this sound, unintelligible yet animal in its excitement, that brought Juliet back to reality. This was not the Damon she knew; the doctor had been replaced by the man and she was not ready for the transformation. The sensations he aroused in her were ones she had not expected to feel for any man except Perry, and she was disgusted with herself.

'Don't!' she cried. 'I'm so ashamed!'

Instantly the movement of his hands was stilled. His mouth lifted from hers and he raised his head, then sat up straight.

'I'm the one who should be ashamed.' His voice, always low, was practically inaudible. 'You were excited from the party and I'm afraid I took advantage of it. You have my word it won't happen again.'

He had gone before she could marshal her thoughts, let alone answer him, and she lay staring into space. Damon had no reason to apologise. Holding her in his arms, he had felt her mounting excitement before she had been aware of it herself, and she could not blame him for responding to it.

Her cheeks burned and she turned her face into the cool linen pillow. Was it only Damon who aroused her, or could any man do the same? She thought of the young banker and the good-looking anaesthetist from the Clinic. Neither of them awakened a spark of desire in her. Yet nor had Damon until he had touched her. Agitated, she sat up. Her legs had recovered their power and she began to undress. Scarlet was a good colour for her. How astute of Damon to suggest she wear it.

To Juliet's surprise—for it was Sunday—Damon had left for the Clinic when she went downstairs to breakfast next morning. She was still ashamed of the way she had behaved last night, and knew she wouldn't be able to relax until she had spoken to him and seen his attitude to her.

In the theatrical world a few kisses, no matter how passionate, were not regarded as important. Indeed, people entered into the most intimate of relationships on the slightest acquaintance and parted as casually as they came together. But Juliet was conditioned by the moral code of her grandparents, and only with Perry had she come near to disregarding it.

She had no means of knowing how Damon felt about last night. He was so controlled that it was not until he had kissed her that she had realised the depth of his passion. More than ever she was astonished that he should have reached his late thirties and still remained a bachelor. She remembered him telling her he had had the occasional affair, but somehow she could not see this as a satisfactory outlet for him.

Pensively she poured a cup of coffee. Until now she

had never analysed her feelings for Damon, but doing so, she saw there were many depths to their relationship of which she had been unaware.

Ali came soft-footed across the grass towards her. She was sitting at a table set under a dwarf palm, shaded from the early morning sun by its large, leafy fronds. This was the best part of the day, when the air was still fresh and the sun had not yet absorbed the moisture in the atmosphere.

'The master wish to have lunch half hour earlier today, madame. He hope okay with you?'

She nodded, and while Ali cleared the table she took a pen and a sheet of paper from her pocket and made various notes about the formation of the drama society. Even in the cool light of day the idea seemed a good one. She reached the end of the paper and went into Damon's study to find some more. It was here that he kept his most private case histories, and it was from here too that he made his twice-weekly telephone calls to London. Some were to his hospital, some to other doctors, and a few to unspecified men who, when they called him back, never left their names.

There was no paper on the desk and she was turning away when she saw a gold pen lying beside the telephone. Immediately she imagined it between Damon's beautifully-shaped fingers. Without knowing why, she picked it up. It was cool and smooth to the touch. Like Damon. Except that last night he had not been cool. Remembering the heat of his body and the sensuous touch of his hands on her skin, she marvelled that he was able to give such a different impression in public. One day the barrier he had erected around himself would topple and the inner man would emerge. But only when the right woman came into his life. Or had she already done so? Had being in daily contact with Monique made him see her with different eyes?

A deep sigh echoed in the room and Juliet looked round. But she was alone and the sigh had come from herself. Surprised by it, she realised how selfish her attitude was towards Damon. She did not want him, yet she did not like to think of him with another woman.

Trying not to think of him at all, she opened various drawers in search of a writing pad. She found one in the bottom drawer and took it out, but when she went to close the drawer, it stuck. She groped with her fingers into the back to see if something had lodged there, and after careful manipulation drew out a flimsy airmail edition of a British newspaper.

Curiosity made her glance at it. It was ten days old and she riffled through the pages, feeling as if she were reading about a country on another planet. There was the usual catalogue of political doom and private misery, leavened with the usual ubiquitous gossip and glamorous photographs. One of them caught her eye. It was Lilah in a bridal dress.

Heart pounding, Juliet forced herself to read the caption. Lilah had not married Perry after all. She was now Carl Forburg's wife and had temporarily given up her career in order to devote herself to her husband. Meanwhile Perry Langdon, in whose film she had been going to star, had discovered another new talent among the stable of Ciné International actresses.

Juliet smiled. How typical of Perry to be on with the new almost before he was off with the old! His feeling for Lilah was as shallow as his feeling had been for herself. She waited for the usual stab of pain, but it did not come. Incredibly she was no longer hurt by the knowledge that Perry had never loved her. What concerned her most was to find out whether she had ever loved him.

She looked at Lilah's picture and wondered why Damon had not shown it to her. Was he afraid she would leave Doria if she knew Perry and Lilah were no longer together? Did he understand her so little that he thought she would plead with Perry to take her back?

Angered that he might think so, she stormed out of the study, all thoughts of the drama society gone from her mind.

CHAPTER TEN

JULIET was in her room when Damon returned home. She almost did not go out to greet him, but knowing that if she pleaded a headache he would come in to see her, she ran a comb through her hair, made her mouth a blaze of scarlet and went into the living room.

Damon was pouring himself a drink and straightened at her entrance, his smile as friendly as always. But why should she expect him to look any different when his profession frequently made it necessary for him to mask his feelings?

'I hope you didn't mind my changing the lunch hour?' he asked. 'I'm expecting a call from London and I wanted to be here for it.'

'Couldn't they call you at the Clinic?' she asked.

'There isn't the same privacy there.'

'You make it sound very hush-hush.' She kept her voice bright. 'Are you looking after a V.I.P.?'

'I regard all my patients as V.I.P.s.' He sat down. 'This call isn't medical.'

'One of your secret ones, then? Don't look so surprised, I know you get them twice a week.'

'I hadn't realised you thought I was keeping them a secret from you.'

'You've never spoken about them.'

'You've never asked about them.'

She tossed her head, her thick dark hair swinging. 'Even if I were really your wife, I'd never question your phone calls.'

'You *are* my real wife,' he said quietly.

'Don't be funny!'

'I wasn't trying to be.'

Damon sipped his drink and crossed one long leg over the other. He was wearing dark trousers with a pale grey shirt open at the collar. It was unusual to see him without a tie and she had never known him go to the Clinic so informally dressed, even on a Sunday. His dark hair was glossy with health despite the noticeable lines of strain at the corners of his eyes. There was also strain in the set of his mouth, which narrowed the fullness of the lower lip.

'The calls I get each week are from the Foreign Office,' Damon said into the silence. 'A friend of mine there—in a fairly senior position—suggested I keep him informed of the political climate here.'

'You make it sound as if there might be trouble.'

'There might.'

Juliet was startled. 'A revolution?'

'Possibly an invasion.'

'Would you still stay here?'

'I doubt it. If there was war, the Clinic would cease to function.'

'The Sheik would take a pretty dim view if you went back to England.'

'The Sheik may well get there ahead of us.'

She flashed him a look to see if he was joking, but there was no humour on his face and she was suddenly nervous for him. 'You're not in any danger, are you?' she asked.

'Me?' He was surprised. 'No more than any other foreign national.'

'Except that you're known to be a close friend of the Sheik. That might make you a target for kidnapping.'

'I wouldn't worry about it,' he said calmly.

'And you're also a world-famous doctor,' she persisted.

'I'm glad you think so.' His voice was dry as dust. 'I haven't been able to cure *you*, have I?'

She was aware of the angry impotence he felt, and was on the point of reassuring him when she remembered the hidden newspaper.

'Why didn't you tell me Lilah was married?'

'Lilah?' Damon looked so blank that Juliet almost believed he did not know whom she meant.

'Lilah Rhodes,' she said. 'The actress who went to Hollywood with Perry. Her marriage was announced two weeks ago.'

'What makes you think I knew about it?'

'Because you hid the paper from me. I found it in your desk. I wasn't snooping,' she added hastily. 'I was looking for some writing paper and when I opened one of the drawers, I found it.'

'And you thought I'd hidden it?' Understanding was in his voice, though the green flecks in his eyes were unexpectedly acid.

'Yes.'

'Then you have a poorer opinion of yourself than I have. Did you think I was worried that you'd fly out to join your ex-fiancé the minute you knew he was free?'

'Why else did you hide the paper?'

Damon looked at his glass, then set it on the table in front of him. The movement brought his head forward into a slanting ray of sun, and she saw there was not a vestige of grey in it, except where the temples glinted silver.

'There could be one of two reasons why I didn't tell you Miss Rhodes was married. Either the one you assumed, or else that I'd forgotten Miss Rhodes was the young lady who replaced you in Mr Langdon's affections.'

'You don't expect me to believe the last one, do you?'

'Believe what you like,' he said coldly.

Juliet's certainty faltered beneath his scorn and she wished she had not rushed so precipitously into this quarrel. 'Perhaps you didn't tell me because you didn't want to remind me of Perry.'

'That's a more friendly supposition than your earlier one,' he said tonelessly. 'But it doesn't happen to be the truth either. I may have read about Miss Rhodes' marriage—though I can't say I recollect doing so; I don't look at those sort of photographs. But even if I had, I wouldn't have remembered who she was. Actresses like her are ten a penny.'

'I'm an actress too,' Juliet said bleakly. 'I'm glad to know you hold us in such high regard.'

'For God's sake!'

The exclamation—as well as his earlier sarcasm—was so unlike him that she wondered if he was still disturbed by the events of the previous night. But then so was she. That was probably why she had misjudged him.

'I'm sorry, Damon. It was wrong of me to accuse you the way I did. You had no reason to remember Lilah.'

'On the contrary, I'm very grateful to her. She's directly responsible for your being in Doria.'

'That isn't true. Perry's walking out on me had nothing to do with Lilah. He started to draw away from me as soon as he knew I was ill. He's always had a phobia about physical fitness.'

'Are you making excuses for him?' queried Damon.

'Of course not. I was just trying to explain that he'll

never come back to me. Not unless I'm miraculously cured.'

She almost said that even if she were, she wouldn't want Perry. But it was embarrassing to admit her change of heart to Damon when he was looking at her with such cold eyes.

'I'm sorry, for what I said to you earlier,' she repeated. 'Will you forgive me?'

'I don't like the word forgiveness between us.' The bleakness went from his eyes and they were warm again. 'Let's forget this conversation happened.'

The telephone rang before she could reply, and he glanced at his watch, nodded to himself and hurried out.

Juliet wandered to the window. She passed the table where Damon's glass stood and on an impulse picked it up. It was still warm from his touch and there was a faint mark of moisture where he had put his mouth to the rim. She pressed her own mouth to it; then amazed at her action, she hurriedly set it down.

What had made her do such a thing? Because she no longer loved Perry it did not mean she should transfer her love to the next man who entered her life. To do so would be as foolish as it would be unrewarding. Besides, she was too emotionally battered to be sure of her feelings. She needed time to reflect; to make quite sure that what she felt for Perry no longer existed. She tried to think of him as she had last seen him, but his image was blurred. It was Damon who was real.

Tentatively she explored the future, trying to see what it held for her and with whom she would share it if she left Damon. But there was no if about it, was there?

The tinkle of the telephone told her his call had

ended, and with a bright smile she faced him as he came back. She refused to worry about what lay ahead. She would take each day as it came and go where Fate guided her. After all, it couldn't be such a bad Fate when it had already guided her towards this kindest of men.

'Ready for lunch?' he asked.

Juliet wanted to tell him she was ready for a lot of things: ready to face life again, to love another man, to conquer her disability. But all she did was nod and lead the way into the dining-room.

Anxious not to say anything that would make him remember their quarrel, she kept up a light flow of talk about the plays she had selected for the drama society. She was so intent on this that it was not until they reached the fruit course that she realised his replies were monosyllabic and, half-way through a sentence, she faltered to a stop.

'You ... you aren't still angry with me, are you?'

'Angry?'

'For what I said about the newspaper photograph.'

'No, no.' With an effort he gathered his thoughts. 'I was thinking of something else.'

Implicit were the words 'more important', and she was chilled by the knowledge that he did not care whether or not she was sorry for having misjudged him.

'The call I had from London was rather disturbing,' he added abruptly. 'It was from my friend at the Foreign Office. It seems things are hotting up over here.'

'You mean there might be an invasion?'

'It's something we should be prepared for. Don't look so perturbed,' he added. 'We can leave here at a moment's notice.'

Juliet glanced around her, enjoying the sight of the

pleasant room and the garden beyond it. The watered grass was like emerald velvet and gaily-coloured flowers filled the beds which their Arab gardener laboriously tilled. Damon was right when he said it would be easy for them to leave. Nothing here belonged to them and once they had gone, no imprint of their personalities would remain. Just as she would leave no imprint on Damon's life when they too parted.

'Shall we go to the British Club this afternoon?' she ventured, filled with an inexplicable urge to be seen with him.

'I'm afraid I'm busy. I have some cases to discuss with Monique. We don't get time at the Clinic, so I'm going to her apartment. We'll talk there for a while and then I'll take her for a drive. She's seen hardly anything of the country since she's been here.'

'What's there to see except sand?'

'The old part of Kuwan is interesting and she might like to see the ruins at Rubah. Her husband was an amateur archaeologist and she went with him on several digs.'

'A woman of many parts.' The words came out more sharply than Juliet intended, and she went on quickly: 'I wish I had a few more interests. Apart from acting, there's nothing I can do.'

'You arrange flowers beautifully—almost as well as a professional—and you run the house extremely well.'

'With four servants to look after two people? You're trying too hard to be kind.'

Damon studied her, his expression thoughtful. 'There's no reason why you can't come with me this afternoon. I didn't suggest it earlier because I thought you'd be bored listening to us talking shop. But you might enjoy the drive and a second look at the ruins.'

'No, thank you,' she said, wishing he had made the suggestion earlier. But he hadn't, and it showed that he wanted to be alone with Monique.

'What will you do with yourself, then?' he asked.

'Read, write, think.'

'About Langdon?'

She was glad her eyes were on a peach she was peeling, and that he could not see her astonishment. Had she known better, she might almost have thought he was jealous.

'It's a waste of time for me to think of Perry,' she said calmly. 'Some things can never be changed.'

'Don't you believe the clock can be put back? Many women do.'

'Many women are foolish.'

'Men too,' Damon said dryly, and pushed back his chair. 'I must be going. I hope to be home by six.'

With an empty afternoon stretching ahead of her, Juliet remained at the table for a long while after Damon had left. She was in no mood to read, nor did she want to think. But unhappy thoughts could not be kept at bay, and she remembered the way Perry had deserted her, and that Damon, her friend, now preferred the company of a woman in his own profession.

Pushing away her self-pity, she went to her room to write some letters. She still kept in touch with Jock, in whose repertory company she had learned so much. Apart from Damon, he was the only person to whom she had confided her misery at being unable to act again. But he, like Damon, ignored her pessimism, and in his last letter had told her how she could resume her career.

'Television is perfect for you,' he had insisted. 'Particularly now, when plays are video-taped. If your legs

give way they can just roll back the film and reshoot it.
You're insane to kiss your career goodbye after all your
years of work.'

Replying to this, Juliet conceded that he was right.
But if she wanted to follow his advice she should be
doing it now, while her name was still fresh in people's
minds. A year was too long to be out of the limelight.
The longer she stayed away from her old contacts, the
harder it would be to pick them up again. For that
reason alone it would be a good thing if she and Damon
were forced to leave here before his contract termi-
nated.

By four o'clock she was tired of writing and, lacking
the patience to read, went back into Damon's study and
took the old newspaper from the drawer. Unfolding it,
she stared at Lilah's face.

The girl was not her enemy. She had never taken
Perry away. He had gone of his own accord, as he would
always do if a relationship became too demanding. He
was one of the world's takers. Yet it was wrong to con-
demn him completely, for in his own way he was a
giver too. She remembered the long hours he worked;
his ferocious attention to detail; his refusal to com-
promise on perfection. In that respect he was a bit like
Damon. Why did her thoughts always bring her back
to Damon. She was becoming obsessed by him.

Six o'clock came and went, and so did half-past the
hour. Her restlessness grew and because she did not
want Damon to think she was anxious about him, she
went to her room. The sun had sunk beyond the trees;
the fierceness had gone from the day and the electric
blue sky was tinged with purple. Soon a slight breeze
would herald the arrival of evening. Sometimes it was

more than slight, and brought with it a fine spray of sand which would lie across the lawn like rhinestones.

She wandered over to the wardrobe and looked at her clothes, then took out one of her new dresses, a bronze silk with a tiered skirt that undulated sensuously with every movement.

It was a quarter to seven when Damon returned, and hearing voices in the hall, she knew Monique was with him. Not giving herself time to think, Juliet went swiftly out to greet her. The woman looked at soigné as ever and it was difficult to believe she had been for a long drive in the heat.

'Do forgive me for barging in on you like this,' Monique apologised, 'but Damon insisted I came back with him. He thinks I'll be lonely on my own.'

'No, I don't. I just thought you two women would enjoy a gossip.'

'That's a sexist remark,' Monique teased. 'Men enjoy gossiping just as much. Don't you agree, Juliet?'

'Only partly. They do gossip, of course, but not in such a destructive way.'

'My God,' said Damon solemnly. 'What a thing to admit in front of a man!'

'That just shows how much your wife loves you,' Monique said, and linked her arm through Juliet's. 'Is it possible for me to freshen up? I feel sticky as a bun.'

Juliet led the way upstairs to her bedroom.

'We don't have a guest room here,' she apologised, 'so you'll have to use my bathroom.'

Monique washed quickly. She wore no make-up other than lipstick and needed none on her vivid face. A quick flick of the comb through her hair and she was ready, swinging round from the dressing-table mirror to look with bright eyes at Juliet, who was seated on the edge of the bed.

'You should have come with us this afternoon,' she said. 'Rubah is quite remarkable.'

'I'm not keen on ruins,' Juliet shrugged. 'If you'd been going to a picture gallery I'd have come like a shot.'

'You and Damon are well suited, then. He's an inveterate gallerygoer.'

'Is he?'

'Didn't you know?' said Monique.

'I don't know Damon very well. I hardly knew him at all when I married him. Hasn't he told you?'

'No. He doesn't talk about you much.'

'Probably because there isn't much to tell.'

'I refuse to believe that,' Monique said warmly. 'You're just feeling blue. You shouldn't let Damon leave you on your own so often.'

Juliet stared at the older woman. 'Don't you know how I met him?' she blurted out. 'I went to him as a patient because I have some obscure disease which makes my legs give way. Damon says it's rare and incurable but not dangerous. But it put paid to my whole life. I had to give up acting and ... and my fiancé walked out on me. I married Damon because he needed a wife in order to come to Doria.'

A long silence met this sudden outpouring of confidence, and Juliet wished she had not spoken. In telling Monique the truth, she had given the woman a hope that might be false.

'It's a—it's been a very convenient marriage,' she went on hurriedly. 'And it's worked out very well.'

'I suspected there was something strange between

the two of you,' Monique said, as if Juliet had not spoken. 'You always seem to be on the defensive with him.'

'I am,' Juliet agreed.

'You shouldn't be. Damon's the kindest man in the world.'

'I know. That's why I don't want to take advantage of him.'

'He wouldn't let you do that. Don't confuse kindness with sentimentality or sympathy with softness. Damon is neither sentimental nor soft.'

'I wish I knew him as well as you do,' Juliet sighed.

'Why?' Monique asked bluntly. 'You're the one he's married.'

'But you're the one who loves him.'

'Possession is nine-tenths of the law.'

Monique looked so sad as she spoke that Juliet almost told her that when they left Doria, Damon might want to end their marriage. But something kept her silent. She had already said too much.

'Please don't tell Damon that you know why he married me,' she said nervously.

'It's as good as forgotten.'

Monique crossed to the door and as Juliet went to follow, her legs lost all sensation and she slid to the floor. Instantly Monique bent to help her up, but Juliet shook her head.

'Please leave me. I'll be fine in a minute.'

'I'll fetch Damon.'

'No. I don't want him to know each time I fall. There's nothing he can do, and it worries him.'

'He's a doctor, he should be told,' Monique insisted.

'No,' Juliet repeated, and avoided Monique's speculative stare. Movement returned to her legs and she flexed them, then carefully stood up and led the way out.

After dinner, Monique pleaded tiredness and asked for Ali to drive her home.

'I'll take you myself,' said Damon, too quickly for Juliet's liking.

'I wouldn't dream of it,' Monique replied. 'You've done more than enough for one day. I'm quite happy to go with Ali.'

Damon frowned, almost as if Monique had snubbed him, and when she had gone he paced the room several times before finally returning to his chair.

He had changed his clothes after his afternoon out, and looked especially carefree in linen slacks and a fine silk sweater in a mixture of blues and greens. It was a brighter colour than he usually wore and Juliet thought it suited him. She marvelled that no woman had succeeded in capturing him, and for the first time speculated on the affairs he might have had. Had Monique once been his mistress?

'Out with it,' he said humorously. 'I can see a question hovering on your lips.'

She coloured, glad that he could not also see what the question was. 'Am I as obvious as all that?'

'From time to time.'

'I was wondering how you escaped marriage,' she murmured, 'and what type of woman you liked.'

'Liquorice allsorts,' he replied. 'Plenty of variety.'

'You're making fun of me!'

'I'm glad you realise it.'

'Be serious, Damon,' she begged.

'Not this time, I have no intention of discussing my murky past with you.'

He drew in his legs and straightened up, and she was

aware of the material pulling against his thighs. He was a big man but so well co-ordinated that his height and size frequently escaped one's notice. But then one didn't expect a doctor to be clumsy. She half smiled. Clumsy was a word one could never apply to Damon.

'Did you have many affairs?' she ventured. 'You can at least answer *that*.'

'Why the interest in my past?'

She almost said her interest lay in his present and future, but knew it would be fatal. Instead she parried:

'Aren't you interested in what *I* did?'

'I don't believe in looking back—it's generally a fruitless exercise.'

His answer left her vaguely dissatisfied, but before she could comment, a distant explosion rattled the windows.

They were both startled. There was another distant but discernible thump and Juliet's mouth went dry.

'It sounds like . . . as if a bomb went off!'

Damon went smartly to the door. 'It's coming from the city. I'll call the Clinic and see if they know what's going on.'

He was away a short time and came back looking pale beneath his tan.

'It's an invasion,' he said tersely. 'The country south of the capital's been taken over, but the Sheik's army is still in control. I think we'll be safer if we move into the Clinic. This house might be in the direct line of fire.'

Ali came dashing into the room, his dark skin tinged with the green of fear, his eyes enormous.

'We're going to the Clinic,' Damon informed him crisply. 'There's no time to take anything with us except a small bag. Be ready to leave in ten minutes.'

Ali ran out and Damon put his hand on Juliet's forearm and gave it a reassuring squeeze.

'We'll be safe at the Clinic. The Sheik doesn't have a paper army, you know. They'll put up a tough fight.'

Appreciating his effort to comfort her, she hurried away to pack. When she returned to the hall, Damon was already there, a bulging briefcase showing he had spent his time gathering up his medical notes rather than personal belongings. She was on the point of suggesting she collect some clothes for him when three explosions shook the house.

'We must get moving,' Damon opened the front door. 'Ali, where the hell are you?' He glanced round at Juliet. 'I'll give him another minute, then we'll go.'

'He's probably gone to collect his family,' Juliet pleaded.

'The rest of the servants are going in the station wagon,' came the curt reply. 'You didn't think I'd go off and leave them, did you?'

This was exactly what she had thought, and she was ashamed. Damon opened the door wider and stepped outside. Another series of explosions rent the air and jagged flashes of light ripped across the sky like lightning. But this was no heavenly storm; it was man-made destruction. The lights in the house flickered, went off, then came on again.

Juliet felt the strength seeping from her legs. Sometimes they gave way without any warning, but there were times when she knew it was going to happen. She staggered to the staircase and managed to sit on the step before she collapsed.

'Ali's here with the car,' Damon called. 'Come on Juliet, if we——'

The rest of what he said was drowned by a thunderous noise as the sky became alive with aircraft. Simultaneously the sonorous crump of bombs echoed around her and the house reverberated to its foundations. The lights went out, came on again and then faded to half their strength.

Juliet tried to rise, but was still paralysed. The house shook again and the chandelier above her head began to swing on its chain. A crack appeared in the ceiling and a thousand crystal drops shivered ominously. With a superhuman effort she flung herself upon the floor and prayed it would not fall upon her.

'Juliet, come on!'

Damon suddenly appeared in the doorway. He saw the chandelier swinging wildly above her and dived across the hall. Another explosion vibrated around them and the ceiling cracked wide open. The chandelier bore down on them and Juliet screamed.

Damon seemed suspended somewhere above her —almost as though he were flying—then his hands reached out and dragged her forward. They seemed to be moving in slow motion, though Juliet knew this was an illusion of fear, for Damon must have moved incredibly fast. But not fast enough. The edge of the falling chandelier caught the side of his head as he turned. He staggered, gasped, and went down on his knees. Juliet tumbled to the floor, but he kept tight hold of her, flinging himself across her as the walls of the house caved in.

Everything seemed to be falling down on top of them, but Damon's body protected her. Another explosion shook the ground and something sharp dug into her temple. The lights were out but brilliant points of white flashed in front of her, turning into a kaleidoscope of colour before everything went black.

CHAPTER ELEVEN

HANDS tugging at her shoulders and a voice entreating her to open her eyes brought Juliet back to consciousness. For a brief instant she thought it was Damon talking, then she saw it was Ali.

Panic-stricken, she struggled to sit up. A lighted candle glimmered on the floor and by its feeble glow she saw Damon lying beside her, his body still partially covering her. He was unconscious and the thin red line of liquid trickling down from his head told her why.

'Quick, Ali, help me to move Dr Masters!'

The young Arab gripped Damon by the shoulders, and as he took the weight, Juliet was able to wriggle free.

'Don't lay him flat,' she said sharply, as Ali went to do so. Somewhere she remembered reading that if a person was unconscious they should always be turned on to their side.

Luckily she could now move her legs and she staggered up. The violent explosions had stopped, though there was still the drone of aircraft and the continuing sound of mortar shells. She knelt beside Damon. In his desire to protect her from the falling chandelier he had come in the direct line of its descent. Blood was still seeping through his hair and even in the dimness she saw the greyness of his skin.

The fear that he was dying gripped her like a pincer, making it hard for her to breathe. She put shaking hands to his face. It was cold as ice: as if he were already dead.

'Damon,' she whispered, 'Damon!'

She bent lower and rested her cheek upon his, then drew quickly back, knowing his only chance for survival was for her to get him to the Clinic fast.

'Is the car damaged?' she asked, and as Ali shook his head, she motioned him to help. 'We must get Dr Masters into the back seat and take him to the Clinic.'

'Is dangerous leave house. Bombs still falling.'

'It's just as dangerous to stay here. But if you don't want to come with me, help me to carry the Doctor to the car and I'll drive myself.'

The shame of a woman being braver than he was revived Ali's courage, and he levered Damon into a sitting position and half dragged, half carried him to the car.

It was difficult to get him firmly placed on the back seat and Juliet was afraid he would slide off. Clambering into the back, she cradled Damon's head in her arms in order to protect it, and told Ali to drive as fast as he could.

Twice their way was blocked by burning vehicles, but Ali managed to make a detour. Troops and tanks and armoured cars were everywhere, and she knew that if the Sheiks pennant had not been flying on the bonnet of their own car they would never have got this far unmolested.

'We nearly there, madame!' Ali shouted triumphantly.

Juliet peered through the window. The entire city seemed to be aflame, but the white bulk of the Clinic loomed solidly ahead.

They screeched to a stop at the entrance and Ali

dashed inside. Seconds later he and another man emerged with a stretcher and gently lifted Damon on to it. The ground floor of the Clinic was teeming with people, mainly Dorian women and children who had come there hoping that the concrete building would afford them more protection than their own flimsy homes. Several nurses were moving among them and one of them immediately hurried over to Juliet.

'You look as if you're in need of treatment too,' she said, staring at the livid swelling on the side of Juliet's face, which Damon's body had not managed to protect.

'I'm fine.' Juliet shrugged away the comment. 'Where are they taking my husband?'

'To be X-rayed. How was he injured?'

'A chandelier fell on him. He's been unconscious since then. I—I—do you think he's dying?'

'People are often unconscious for hours from the smallest blow,' the nurse said, ignoring the question. 'Would you like to go to the X-ray department and wait there?'

'Will they let me?'

'If you insist on it. But don't say I told you. Come, I will take you there.'

An hour later Damon was lying in a small room on the ground floor. It was normally used as an office, but a bed had been wheeled into it, and Juliet knew he had been brought here in case the occupants of the upper floors had to be brought down. If the shelling of the city continued, there was every likelihood that the Clinic would be evacuated completely.

No one seemed to know what was happening and Juliet was too shattered by the events of the last couple of hours to care. All her thoughts were centred on Damon. She sat beside his bed, occasionally touching his cold hand. His face looked different with his eyes closed. It made her notice the well-chiselled features. He had the head of a poet but the body of a man who could hew marble. In his own way Damon was a sculptor too, but instead of giving life to inanimate substances, he gave it to sick people.

She prayed for his recovery, knowing that if he died she would want to die too. The knowledge did not surprise her. It was as if she had known it for a long time but had been unwilling to admit it. Now her inhibitions had gone, and she knew that to love Damon was as natural to her as breathing.

'Oh, darling,' she said tremulously, kissing his fingers. 'Darling Damon! If only I'd told you what you mean to me!'

Pulling her chair forward, she remained close beside him. His breathing was so faint as to be almost imperceptible and her heart began to race with fear. What if he were dying and they hadn't told her? She put her lips to his. They were warm and soft and she was reassured.

A hand touched her shoulder and with a start she lifted her head and saw Monique. The woman's face was drained of colour and her eyes were dark pools of anxiety as she regarded the man in the bed.

'I just heard about Damon,' she said. 'It's taken me all this time to get here from my apartment. The roads are blocked every inch of the way.'

'Have you spoken to the doctor who took the X-rays?' Juliet asked. 'He said Damon would be all right, but——'

'He is,' Monique reassured her. 'Look, he's stirring already.'

He was; muttering inaudibly and moving his hands

on the coverlet. Then with startling suddenness he opened his eyes. For an instant they were blank, then recognition came into them and he tried to sit up.

'No, you don't,' said Monique, pushing him back again. 'You must lie still for twenty-four hours.'

'Like hell I will!'

'Like hell you will,' Monique agreed. 'So relax and show me that you know when to give in.'

Damon stared into Monique's face, apparently oblivious of Juliet's presence.

'I'm glad you're safe,' he said quietly. 'I was afraid you might be trapped in the suburbs. I tried to phone you from the house, but the lines were down. If——'

'You're talking too much,' Monique cut in. 'Be quiet and rest.'

'Where's Juliet?'

'On the other side of you.'

Carefully Damon turned his head and Juliet came into his line of vision. 'You aren't hurt, are you?'

'You made sure of that,' she said shakily, and touched his hand.

She felt him flinch and she quickly drew her hand away, shaken by the knowledge that he could not bear her touch. Was it because these last few weeks in Monique's company had shown him what the French-Canadian meant to him? She glanced at Monique and saw she was watching Damon with professional concern.

'I'll prescribe a sedative for you,' Monique informed him. 'And nothing to eat until tomorrow. But you can have as much liquid as you want.'

'Thanks, doctor. But all I want is to know what's going on here. Are all the staff in?'

'Every one of them. The top floor has been cleared

because of rockets and the patients have been taken to other wards. We have about forty beds free.'

'That's excellent. Has there been any official word from anyone?'

'No. But according to the radio, the army is holding its own.'

'They've got to do more than that.'

'Will the British intervene?' Juliet asked.

'We won't do anything to fan the flames of this particular fire.' Damon's voice was fainter. 'I wonder if there's a chance of my getting a call through to London?' He looked at Monique. 'Would you bring a phone in for me?'

'No.'

He sat up and flung back the sheet, at the same time setting his feet to the ground. He staggered, swore loudly and clutched hold of Monique before falling back on to the bed.

'Now will you stay where you are?' she demanded.

'Only until I get my strength back, so stop playing the sergeant-major and get me a telephone.'

Silently Monique went out and Damon sighed and eased himself up on the pillow. 'My head feels as if it's exploding. I suppose the chandelier fell on me?'

'The edge of it. If you'd been a little further under it, it would have killed you.' Juliet's voice wobbled and he made an impatient gesture with his hand.

'Well, I wasn't, and it didn't. So no tears, please. A day in bed and I'll be good as new.'

'You can't blame me for being upset,' she said. 'You were hurt because you wanted to save me.'

'I acted instinctively.' His eyes had been half closed, but he opened them fully and regarded her without expression. 'Psychologists say that in times of stress one reverts to one's upbringing. I daresay that applied to me tonight: women and children first and all that sort of thing. Call it the British boarding-school syndrome.'

She knew he was trying to make it clear that he had not saved her because she meant anything to him—other than being a defenceless woman. But it did not lessen her love for him nor the debt she owed him. Tears welled into her eyes and he saw their glitter and looked impatient, turning with obvious relief to Monique who had come back with a telephone and was plugging it into the wall.

Juliet went to sit on a nearby chair and watched the scene as if it were a tableau. But that was how she felt: an onlooker watching two people who were so right for each other that it was incredible they had not come together before.

Amazingly quickly Damon was connected to his Foreign Office friend. The conversation was impossible for her to follow and she had the impression they were speaking in a deliberately cryptic way. This was confirmed when the call ended and he informed them that though the Sheik was still in control, the army of Bendam, the neighbouring country on Doria's northern border, was coming to his aid.

'Bendam's half the size of Doria,' Monique expostulated. 'It's like a gnat coming to the aid of a flea!'

'Anything is better than nothing,' said Damon. 'The United Nations Security Council has called for an emergency meeting and there's every likelihood they'll send in their own troops. But for the moment we should remain where we are.'

'Which endorses my order to you,' Monique stated,

and then smiled at Juliet. 'You should be lying down too. You're a pretty shade of yellow.'

'I feel fine,' Juliet insisted.

'Go and lie down,' Damon ordered brusquely. 'I don't need you fussing over me.'

'You see?' said Monique. 'You're not needed.'

The words could not have been more apt, and Juliet rose and followed Monique out.

'There's a small room next door to this one where you can lie down,' the woman said, opening a door as she spoke.

Juliet found herself in what was evidently an examination room. Apart from the usual high couch there was a small truckle bed, and it was here that she settled, suddenly accepting the fact that she was exhausted.

'I'm sorry I can't offer you a proper bed,' Monique apologised, 'but we're bursting at the seams with casualties.'

'I thought you said you had forty beds free.'

'I lied. I didn't want Damon to worry. It's my guess that we'll all be evacuated from here within the next forty-eight hours.' She flicked off the centre light as she spoke and left only a small lamp burning.

'Where are *you* going to sleep?' Juliet enquired.

'The operative word is "when".'

'Isn't there something I can do to help? I can't lie here doing nothing.' Juliet jumped up as she spoke, then abruptly collapsed on the bed. 'Damn my legs!' she cried. 'I feel so useless!'

'Please don't be upset,' Monique said in a gentle voice, 'but you do see it's impossible for you to help us.'

She went out and Juliet lay on the hard bed, tears

coursing down her cheeks. There were many things that were impossible, and her useless legs only one of them. No wonder Damon treated her as a little girl who needed to be cared for, and not as a wife.

'Even if I were well, I wouldn't be his wife in the real sense,' Juliet whispered aloud. 'Our marriage is a business contract and I can't change the terms even though I've changed the way I feel.'

She thought of Perry, but he no longer had substance. Damon was the man in her life, though he did not know it; must never know it unless he himself showed that he wanted to change the situation. It seemed so unlikely that she was filled with despair, and turning her face into the pillow, she wept.

The sky was still dark when she awoke, but already the clinic was humming with activity. Most of the nurses she saw looked pale and haggard, as if they had been up all night. The main hall was covered with mattresses and were already occupied by wounded people. An orderly was walking round, dispensing coffee, and Juliet took a cup.

'Do you know where Dr Lamont is?' she asked.

'She was here until about an hour ago,' the young man informed her, 'then she disappeared. She's probably gone to have a rest.'

Juliet thanked him and went back along the corridor. She would see how Damon was, then get some breakfast.

She went into his room, stopping in surprise as she saw Monique there. The woman was sitting by Damon's bed, her head resting on the side of the mattress, her auburn hair splaying out to within an inch of his hand. She was fast asleep, as was Damon.

Tentatively Juliet moved forward, but neither the

man nor the woman heard her. Damon was not as pale as he had been last night and the white bandage around his head made his skin look darker.

Quietly she went out. It was fitting that Monique had gone to Damon's room to rest. It illustrated how close they had become since working together. If her own love for Damon had come to fruition before Monique had come back into his life, she might have stood a chance of awakening his interest in her. But how could she compete with a woman who was able to talk to him on equal terms about his work; who had the charm of sophistication and maturity?

'Madame, please!' She jerked round and saw Ali hurrying towards her. He was holding her case and Damon's. 'I want give you these last night, but I not find you. Each time I look, I given something to do.'

Seeing his unshaven face and the bloodstains on his suit, she gave him a reassuring smile. 'Dr Masters will be delighted that you were able to do something useful.'

'Perhaps he take me to England. You leaving soon, yes?'

'I'm not sure.'

'All foreigners going.' Ali looked at her with pathos. 'You please ask master let me go with you? I eat little and work hard.'

'Oh, Ali, if we don't take you it won't have anything to do with your eating too much.' Juliet was almost near to tears. 'I promise I'll tell my husband what you said, but I can't promise that we'll be able to take you.'

He glanced at the door behind her. 'Is the master there?'

'Yes, but he's asleep.' Juliet thought of Monique's head on the bed and quickly began to walk down the corridor, Ali following at her heels like an anxious puppy.

After a quick breakfast in the kitchen on the lower ground floor, Juliet went to the wards to see if there was anything she could do, and soon found herself cutting up sheets to make bandages. Every hour more and more wounded were brought in and she caught a glimpse of Monique as she bent down to look at a stretcher case, her hair a deeper red against her pale skin.

Juliet realised she had not spoken to Damon this morning and knew he would consider it strange if she did not visit him. She kept seeing an image of Monique's head resting near his hand, and wondered if he had touched her hair or put his hands to her face. Pushing such painful thoughts aside, she almost ran down the corridor to his room. He was sitting up in bed, holding a mirror in one hand and unwinding the bandage from his head with the other.

'You shouldn't be taking it off,' she exclaimed, and moved forward to stop him.

Irritably he shook away her hand. 'I'm a doctor, Juliet. I wouldn't tell you how to act on the stage, would I?'

Instantly she subsided. 'Perhaps I'd better find Monique. Maybe she can persuade you.'

'I've already seen Monique and she knows I'm getting up.'

'You haven't any clothes.'

'Ali brought them in to me.'

'You've got everything organised, haven't you?' she said crossly.

'Everything.'

'You saved my life last night,' she said abruptly.

'Each time I think of it I——'

'We've already discussed it,' he interrupted. 'Stop fussing over me and leave me alone.'

Hurt, she stepped back.

'I didn't mean that the way it sounded,' Damon apologised. 'But I assume you won't want to stay here while I wash down.'

She went scarlet and, seeing his sardonic smile, said sharply: 'Wouldn't it be better if you got someone to help you? I know you only had a *minor* bang on the head, but you *are* still suffering from it.'

'I have no intention of letting a nurse wash me.'

'Shall I ask Monique to help you?' Juliet said without expression.

'Not unless you want me to throttle you.' A glint came into his eyes. 'On second thoughts, Monique might do very well.'

'Isn't excitement dangerous for a person with concussion?'

The glint intensified. 'Monique was your suggestion, not mine.'

Silently he pushed aside the sheet and, recognising his determination, she left him alone. But she remained outside the door, every moment expecting to hear him fall. There was no sound and her tension increased. It had almost reached explosive point when he emerged, impeccable in dark slacks and a blue shirt. He was struggling into a white jacket and she looked at him in surprise.

'I didn't know consultants wore those,' she blurted out.

'They don't. But I've an idea I won't be doing my usual work around here.'

As if to reinforce his statement, a series of explosions

erupted in the surrounding district, followed by a burst of machine-gun fire that came from somewhere uncomfortably close.

'You'll be glad to know that my friend at the Foreign Office assured me everything is under control here,' Damon said wryly. 'If things get even more under control, I'll have to get you out of the country.'

Juliet started to say she had no intention of leaving without him, when the entire building shook. Glass shattered everywhere and there were several high pitched screams.

'Bomb blasts,' Damon muttered. 'Can't the bastards see the Red Cross we've painted on the roof?'

He began to run down the corridor, then staggered and leaned on the wall. He had lost all the colour from his face and he put his hand to his head as if in pain. Juliet knew better than to comment on it, but remained silently beside him until he recovered sufficiently to walk again. This time he went more slowly, and his colour had seeped back as he reached the first floor.

All the wards were full and patients were lying in the corridor. Quickly Damon went from one to another. A young male orderly come over and gave him a stethoscope, but though he hung it around his neck, he used it infrequently. He seemed to rely more on his hands, which he would place on a body and hold there for several seconds.

'He's an instinctive doctor,' the orderly murmured.

There was a tightening in Juliet's throat and her love for Damon burgeoned so intensely that she was afraid she might not be able to hide it.

Throughout the day he worked ceaselessly. Juliet offered her services to anyone who could use them, but aware that she might fall without warning, she did not carry dishes or anything breakable. The afternoon she found herself entertaining a group of children, and seeing the way she kept them enthralled, the nurses brought more and more to her.

Some of them understood a little English and they explained the stories she was telling to those who didn't. Racking her distant memories, she recounted farmyard tales, and soon the children were vying with each other to copy the sounds she was making, until the room was a cacophony of dogs barking, cats mewing and goats bleating.

Juliet remained with the children until they had been settled for the night. They were pathetically grateful for her attention, and realising that many of them were now orphans, she was filled with hatred for the men who had made them so.

It was nine o'clock before they had settled down, and she went exhaustedly in search of Damon, carefully picking her way along the corridors, where mattresses lay almost touching each other. The air was still loud with mortar fire, though not as loud as it had been during the day, and she knew that soon it would cease and not start up again until the morning.

Suddenly Damon was beside her. He was grey with fatigue and she wished she had the right to hold him close and show her concern. Instead she kept her voice level as she spoke.

'Don't you think you've done enough for one day?'

'That goes for both of us. You look like I feel.'

'I'm too tired to care,' she admitted. 'I'm just going to put up my feet and sleep.' They resumed walking. 'How much longer do you think we'll be able to carry on here?'

'God knows. The Sheik is a prisoner in his palace, but the army is still loyal to him and fighting.'

They reached the room where she had spent last night and Juliet saw mattresses and wounded men on the floor. One of them raised his head and looked at her, then gave a half smile to Damon, as if recognising the white jacket.

'You won't be sleeping in here tonight,' Damon said quietly, and shepherded her along the corridor to his own room. Taking a key from his pocket, he unlocked the door, ushered her in and relocked it behind them.

'Where's Monique?' she asked.

'In an ambulance somewhere in the city. She had no right to go out during such gunfire,' he said fiercely, 'but I couldn't stop her.'

'You'd have been in an ambulance too if you hadn't been afraid of collapsing.'

He did not answer, but took off his jacket and stretched painfully, as if to ease his aching muscles. Juliet perched on a chair, terribly conscious that there was only one narrow bed in the room. She could not see Damon letting her spend the night in the chair, and she had no intention of letting him sit up in it either.

'There must be some other place where I can sleep,' she said.

'You can go next door with the patients, or you can try one of the tables in the canteen. The nursing staff have given up their beds, and that's where *they're* dossing down.'

She half rose and he gave an irritable exclamation. 'For heaven's sake, Juliet, what do you think it would look like if you went off to sleep with strangers? You're my wife. People will expect you to stay with me.' He glanced at the narrow bed. 'Couples have managed in

a bed that size before,' he said dryly, 'and I'm in no fit
state to rape you—even if I were so inclined.'

'Which you're not,' she said instantly.

'Which I'm not,' he agreed. 'So do me a favour and
get undressed.'

'There's no point. I'll be all right like this.'

'Take off your dress,' he said abruptly, 'and don't
scream when I take off my shoes. I assure you it's not a
prelude to seduction.'

Turning her back on him, she unbuttoned her dress.
Her hands were shaking and she took longer than
usual to do it. Then she went over to the wash basin.

'There's a clean towel in one of the drawers,' Damon
said.

She took it out and washed and dried her face before
moving over to the bed. She tried not to watch Damon,
but was aware of him at the sink. He washed with slow,
deliberate movements and she noticed the graceful
curve of his body as he bent over the basin. His hair
fell forward and, as he straightened, he pushed it back
with impatient fingers, wincing as they came in contact
with his injured skull.

'I've a bump on my head the size of an egg,' he muttered, and came over to the bed. He had loosened his
shirt and several buttons were undone. 'Get in,' he said
brusquely, 'and don't take more than half of it.'

She obeyed him and lay back on the pillow. There
were two and she had spread them out so that they
could each have one. Damon eased himself up beside
her and the bed creaked beneath his weight. He looked
immensely tall, viewed from this angle, and she was
conscious of his thigh pressing into hers and his shoulder digging into her breast. She knew the bed was too
narrow to accommodate them both if they lay flat, and

she turned on her side and found herself on the very edge of the bed.

'You'll fall out if you're not careful,' he said in amusement.

'Not if you can give me an inch more room.'

'I can do better than that.' He turned fully on his side, facing inwards because this was the only way he could avoid lying on the tender part of his skull. His breath was warm upon the nape of her neck and she knew that if he held her close it would be far less uncomfortable for them both. Yet she dared not suggest it, even though every fibre of her body wanted him.

'I do wish you'd relax,' he said quietly. 'You're as tense as a coiled spring. I've already told you you're quite safe with me. You're not my type.'

She knew he was trying to put her at her ease, but his remark could not have been more hurtful. She was still thinking what to say in reply when she heard him give a deep indrawn breath and knew he had fallen asleep.

She longed to turn and look at him, but was scared of disturbing him. Instead she inched inwards a little and closed her eyes. Dear Damon! How unstintingly he had offered to help her when she had needed him most. But it was as nothing compared with how much she needed him now. And it was too late to tell him.

CHAPTER TWELVE

DAMON put out his hand to touch the rich dark brown hair on the pillow beside him. It was as glossy as if it had been polished with a silk handkerchief. And it felt like silk too, the way her skin had felt. His pulses quickened and he moved closer to her. He would stay like this for a while and pretend she was really his. Maybe he could even hold her. If she woke up she would think he was still sleeping. He closed his eyes and slowly put his hand upon her waist, letting his arm go heavy, as if it were an unconscious movement.

Instantly he felt her tense and knew his touch had awakened her. He kept his hand where it was and waited for her reaction. Her whole body trembled and he felt her ease away from him and slide off the bed.

He kept his eyes closed. Well, he had his answer— if he had needed one. Even though she believed he had touched her in his sleep, she could not bear it. How would she react if he told her he loved her? She was already embarrassed because he had kissed her the other night, and if she knew that the kiss stemmed from love and not desire, then compassion would be added to embarrassment. And he was damned if he wanted her pity. Anything else but that.

Feigning a yawn, he opened his eyes. Juliet was at the sink but she heard him stir and turned to give him a faint smile. How beautiful she looked with her flushed cheeks and her hair in disarray. Damon glimpsed the curve of her breasts above her bra and

157

saw the shoulder strap cutting into the smoothness of her shoulder. If only he had the right to pull the strap down and press his lips to the mark it would leave; then to undo the fastenings and hold those soft warm breasts in his hands; to savour their sweetness against his lips and bury his face in their fullness.

He sat up, the sharpness of his movement making his head throb. It was a good thing he was still under the weather. If he weren't, he might not have left her alone last night. In times of stress one frequently felt the need to love another person, but never had he felt it as much as now. He thought of his life without Juliet, and knew he would never feel as strongly about anyone else again. There was a rap on the door and Juliet shot him a nervous glance and then went over and unlocked it. It was Monique, looking amazingly bright and trim.

'Anything wrong?' Damon asked sharply.

'All Europeans and Americans are being airlifted out of Kuwan. We've been ordered to go to the airfield at once.'

'Civilians, yes.' Damon glanced at Juliet. 'But I'm not going.'

'You must,' said Monique. 'United Nations troops are flying in. Some are already here and all foreign residents have to leave.'

'I'm staying with my patients,' he insisted.

'Then I'll stay too. And so will the rest of the Western staff.'

'Fine.'

'I'll also stay,' said Juliet. 'I'm your wife.'

Damon eyed her silently, knowing that this was the very best reason for her to go. To have her within reach—where he could see her and touch her—was more than he could tolerate. The work ahead of him was going to be harrowing enough without putting himself through any additional emotional trauma.

'You're the last person in the world I want to have here,' he said brusquely. 'You've got to go.'

Turning his back on her, he went to the sink and splashed cold water on his face. When he straightened, only Monique was with him, standing by the door and looking at him with a strange expression.

'Take that look off your face,' he said. 'The last thing I want is sympathy.'

'You love her,' Monique stated. 'I don't know why I didn't see it before. I'm so used to thinking you immune to women that it never dawned on me—particularly when Juliet said you only married her because she was ill.'

Half-way out of the room, Damon stopped in his tracks. 'She *told* you?'

'Yes. I think she felt the need to confide in someone.'

'Well, don't *you* do any confiding. I don't want her to know how I feel.'

'Why not?'

'Because I don't want her to stay with me out of gratitude—and that's all she feels. You know her illness is incurable, don't you?'

'All the more reason to tell her you love her. She needs you, Damon.'

'I don't want to be needed in that way.' His voice was harsh. 'My patients need me. Every sick and suffering soul that comes to see me needs me. The last thing I want is to have a wife who needs me for the same reason.'

'She may grow to love you.'

'When she jumps a mile if I go near her?'

'She's nervous of you.'

'Spare me the fiction!' He walked down along the corridor and Monique kept up with him, half running to match his stride. 'What time does the airlift begin?' he demanded.

'As of now.'

'Then make sure Juliet gets away.'

'*You* should do that. You're her husband.'

Damon quickened his pace. With Juliet gone he might find some peace. He would concentrate entirely on his work. In the past it had been more important to him than anything else and he would make it so again.

He reached the main hall and inched his way between mattresses to where Juliet was sipping some coffee.

'Get to the airport,' he said sharply. 'I wasn't joking about it.'

'I know.' She did not look at him. 'You can't bear the sight of me, can you?'

He caught his breath, feeling as if she had dealt him a physical blow. 'This isn't the time or place for such a discussion.'

'Then I'll leave at once.' Like a child who had been given orders by a strict parent, Juliet set down her cup.

'Don't forget your case,' he said. 'I'll get Ali to bring it for you.'

Swinging round, he searched the room for a sight of his young manservant and spied him at the far end. 'Ali!' he called, and the boy came running. Damon turned to Juliet and found her gone. With a curse he made for the door. He reached it in time to see a jeep pulling away from the front steps. A crowd of civilians was in it and Juliet was among them.

'Juliet,' he called. *'Darling!'*

She did not hear him, though she saw him and raised her hand. He knew she had deliberately left this way in order to avoid speaking to him again and, remembering his brusqueness, he did not blame her.

He stood on the steps until the jeep was out of sight, taking with it the person he loved above all else. Then straightening his shoulders he went back into the Clinic.

Juliet remembered little of her journey to London. The aircraft was a large one and was completely filled by oil executives and their wives and children.

She knew she should have said something to Damon before leaving, but his sharp tone had brought her close to breaking point and, rather than let him see it, she had taken the easy way out.

It was only as the plane approached the British coast that she remembered she had nowhere to stay. Expecting to be in Doria for a year, she had given up her flat. She wished she had thought to ask Damon where she should stay, yet even trying to hold the most banal conversation with him had become difficult, and she was not sure why.

Had the realisation that she loved him put her so much on the defensive that Damon had misconstrued it as dislike? Or had she reacted to a subtle change in his own attitude towards her—a change brought about by his growing closeness with Monique? Thinking about the past few weeks, she recollected many occasions when he had not returned home for lunch, but had chosen to have it with the French-Canadian. He had always given pressure of work as the reason, and though she had at first believed him, she had gradually seen it as an excuse not to be with her.

His behaviour at the Clinic last night had crystal-lised her belief that he did not like her. That was why he had been so sarcastic. The Damon of a few months ago would have made a joke at having to share a bed with her, and would not have lain beside her as tense as a ramrod. It was this that had made her so ashamed of the deep desires which she felt for him.

If only she could dislike him; if only she could blame him for wanting to terminate their agreement before the year was up. Yet she couldn't. When he had offered her his name he had not known that Monique's return into his life would make him regret his pre-cipitate marriage. Well, he need not regret it any longer. She would write and tell him to get an annul-ment whenever he wished.

Meanwhile she had to find somewhere to live. She would book into a small hotel and then contact one of her girl friends; she was bound to find someone who could put her up temporarily. Then she would see her agent and find out if he could get her some radio work.

Her depression lifted slightly as she started to plan her future. Life would go on without Damon. It wasn't going to be easy, but she was determined to cope on her own.

It was not until the plane landed and Juliet saw the bevy of photographers at the barrier that she knew their return from Doria was a newsworthy item. She loathed the prospect of facing inquisitive reporters and hung back in the hope that the other passengers would satisfy the newshounds sufficiently for them to leave her alone.

'Mrs Masters?' A steward beckoned her as she

reached the exit of the plane. 'There's a van waiting for you at the bottom of the stairs with a wheelchair.'

'I don't need a wheelchair!' Juliet exclaimed.

'We were told you have difficulty in walking. A message was relayed to the Captain during the flight.'

She knew immediately that Damon had organised the call, and marvelled that he had managed to communicate with England at a time like this. But then he had the ear of the Sheik.

'I can manage on my own, thank you,' she repeated, and walked down the steps to prove it. Luckily her legs did not let her down and she braced herself for the walk across the tarmac.

'Mrs Masters?' This time her name was spoken by a man of medium height, in his middle thirties. His pin-striped suit, Eton tie and drawling voice revealed his background. 'I'm Bruce Halford—a friend of Damon's from the Foreign Office.'

'I suppose he asked you to meet me? I feel very guilty about it.'

'There's no need. It's a pleasure.'

He guided her round to the far side of the aircraft where a small saloon was unobtrusively parked. As soon as they were both inside, he shot smartly down the runway.

'Sorry about the speed,' he apologised, giving her a quick glance, 'but if I don't take advantage of the element of surprise we'll have a pack of reporters on our tail.' He looked into his driving mirror and nodded. 'Some of them have already seen us, but we've got too much of a start on them.'

They were approaching a high wire fence, the gates in the middle of it guarded by police. Slowing down, Bruce Halford took a disc and photograph from his pocket, held it up to the window and was immediately waved forward. They drove out of the airfield and along a narrow country lane that eventually led them to the motorway.

'Now we're safe,' he said with relief. 'I didn't think you'd appreciate being bombarded with questions so soon after your return.'

'How right you are!'

'Mind you, I have a few of my own,' he apologised. 'Damon was very terse when he called me.'

'He's inundated with wounded,' Juliet explained. 'Part of the Clinic has been shelled and the top floor is unusable. They're running short of medical supplies and with the other hospital out of action, the Clinic is getting all the casualties.'

'It must be hell,' Bruce Halford said. 'But the U.N. are sending in medical staff and drugs. I've already notified Damon.'

Juliet made no comment. A signpost told her they were reaching London and her apprehensions returned. 'I feel like a refugee. I left all my clothes behind and I've nowhere to stay.'

'That's another thing Damon told me,' Bruce Halford said. 'In the rush of your departure he forgot to mention that his Harley Street house is open. He cabled your housekeeper a week ago to close the cottage and come back to town. He's full of foresight, your husband. He knew all this was brewing and laid his plans accordingly. He also cabled one of his sisters to meet you at your home, and I'm sure she'll bring some clothes along for you. Certainly enough to tide you over for a day or two.'

Clever Damon, Juliet thought wryly. He had made plans for every contingency except that of falling in love with another woman. She sighed, and though she was not in the least tired, decided that to pretend fatigue was an excellent way of avoiding any discussions with her sister-in-law. Which one of them was Betty Ingram? Damon's three sisters had been difficult to distinguish and her meeting with them had taken place when she was too preoccupied with her own distress to take notice of anyone else.

She hoped Betty was the youngest one, and was disappointed when she entered the house in Harley Street to find she was the eldest. However, she was charming, efficient and understanding.

'Bath, bed, a light meal and a long sleep,' she said crisply. 'We'll have plenty of time for talking tomorrow.'

CHAPTER THIRTEEN

JULIET inserted the key in the lock and opened the front door. As always, the small hall, shiny with copper pots and warm with red-brown Turkish rugs, welcomed her home.

Her own home. Three months ago she would gladly have settled for a bed-sitter or a shared apartment, but events had moved swiftly and happily for her since her return to England.

Though Bruce Halford had kept the reporters at bay at the airport, she eventually had to face them. Damon's decision to remain at the Clinic despite the war raging around him had brought him into the limelight, and when he had firmly refused to speak to the press, they had hounded his wife.

Juliet agreed to see them at Damon's house in Harley Street, and had gently explained that her husband remained at the Clinic in order to show his belief in the Sheik, whose democratic and enlightened rule would triumph over dictatorship.

'My husband doesn't believe that a nation is conquered simply because its territory is overrun. It is the will of the people that counts, and *they* want the Sheik Quima.'

Juliet's picture appeared in several of the papers and she was asked to talk on television about her experiences during the invasion. She hated every moment of the limelight and did not realise that the blaze of publicity would help her career until Lew Morgan, her agent, rang her one morning to say he had been inundated with offers of work for her.

'Your appearance on the Craig Show did it,' he said. 'You looked like an angel and you talked like a dream. There are at least three good offers you can choose from.'

'I'd better come to see you,' said Juliet, and did so that very afternoon.

Lew was one of the most successful agents in the business. He was talkative yet gave away no secrets, and knowing she could trust his discretion, she told him of her illness and of her marriage.

'I don't know how much longer my marriage will last, and it's important for me to be self-supporting. I realise the theatre is out, but maybe you can find me some work in television. I know it won't be easy, but I'm willing to take *any* part, no matter how small. Even something on radio.'

'You're too beautiful to be hidden. You'd also make less money on radio.' Lew eyed her. 'Is your marriage definitely over?'

'Yes.'

'Do you know Perry's going to direct his second picture in London? Ciné are so delighted with him that they've doubled his budget. He's got it made this time.'

'The Perrys of this world generally have,' she shrugged.

'Don't be bitter, sweetheart. You'll get lines on your face.'

'I'm not bitter,' she told him. 'Just more sceptical about human nature than I was a year ago.'

'Would you take a part in Perry's picture if I could get you one?'

Juliet considered the idea, then nodded. 'I don't see

why not. He means nothing to me as a man, but he's a great director.'

'If he finds that you're indifferent to him, he might see it as a challenge to get you back.' Lew's shrewd eyes narrowed. 'What chance would he have?'

'None. I've changed, Lew. Perry isn't my type any more.'

It was this conversation which Juliet remembered as she went into the kitchen to make herself supper. The last few weeks had been busy ones. She had been offered a leading part in a television play and Lew had given her such a generous advance when she signed her contract that she had been able to rent this well-furnished flat in Chelsea.

Tonight she felt almost too tired to eat. She had spent the day rehearsing at the television studios, and had turned down her co-star's invitation to have dinner with him. But it was more than tiredness that had made her do so: it was the boredom that always assailed her the moment any man stopped talking shop and tried to talk personally. It was then that she always found herself comparing her escorts with Damon, and none of them matched up to him.

Foolishly she had believed that when she left Harley Street she would be able to forget him. But he was constantly in her mind, permeating every thought, every action. It wasn't the television director she tried to please in her most difficult scenes, but Damon, who seemed to be out there in the ether, watching her. It did not seem normal to be so obsessed with a man, and she had confided her fears to Diana, her closest girl friend.

'You're crazy all right,' was Diana's comment. 'Crazy about your husband. It's time you faced up to it.'

'And do what?'

'Tell him how you feel.'

'He'd die of embarrassment. Anyway, there'd be no point. Monique is much more suitable for him than I am.'

'So how come he didn't ask *her* to marry him?'

'Because he hadn't seen Monique for more than a year, and her husband was alive then. It wasn't until she came to work with him in Doria that he realised how he felt.'

'He never told you so,' Diana stated. 'Perhaps you're wrong.'

'You didn't see them together, the way I did.'

'Okay, so he talked to her about his work. But that doesn't mean he loves her. You're younger than Monique, and you're surely more beautiful. You should have fought for him.'

'Youth and beauty wouldn't influence Damon,' said Juliet.

'He's a man, isn't he?'

'Of course he is. But he wouldn't love a woman simply because of her looks.' Juliet sighed heavily. 'I thought that once I was away from him I'd forget him, but I feel even worse.'

'Give yourself more time—and date other men, even if they bore the pants off you. Lay new memories over your old ones, Juliet. That's one way of keeping them buried.'

But Juliet had ignored Diana's advice and decided that her main solace would be work. She still frequently lost all sensation in her legs, but had learned to adjust to it; the scald she had given her leg in Doria serving as a constant reminder to use a trolley for carrying things.

She did this with the pizza and coffee she had prepared, and wheeled it into her cosy sitting-room.

As she ate her supper she thought of the work Lew
had lined up for her. There were two more television
plays to do and he had asked her to play the feminine
lead in a thirteen-part serial set in the eighteenth
century.

'I'm not sure it's wise for me to get type-cast in a
serial,' she had protested, but Lew had assured her
otherwise.

'It's only for thirteen episodes, and it will help to
make your name known to millions of viewers.'

But she was still not sure she wanted to do it, and
debated whether to speak to Jock. She poured out her
coffee and switched on the television, keeping the
sound low.

Suddenly Damon's face appeared on the screen. The
coffee cup shook in her hand and she set it on the
trolley and leaned forward to turn up the sound.
Damon's voice, deep as she remembered it, floated into
the room.

'Naturally I'm pleased to be home,' he was saying. 'I
had planned to remain in Doria for a year, but Dr
Lamont has taken over for me. She is a close and
trusted colleague and has the loyalty of the staff.'

Damon's praise of Monique renewed Juliet's jeal-
ousy of her, and she could not understand why
Monique was staying in Doria when Damon was in
London.

The telephone rang and she nearly jumped out of
her skin. Yet it couldn't be Damon calling her. He was
on the television screen in front of her. She picked up
the receiver, relaxing as she heard Diana's voice.

'Did you know your husband was back?'

'Dr Masters is back,' Juliet retorted. 'He was never my husband.'

'Cut the semantics, will you, and tell me if you're going to see him?'

'No. If he wants to see me, he knows where I am. When I moved here I sent him my address, but I never heard from him.'

'Ring him, Juliet.'

'No!' Juliet was sharp. 'Look, I must go now. I've some new lines to learn. I'll call you later in the week.'

For the rest of the evening Juliet sat close to the telephone, and only at midnight did she concede that Damon was not going to call her. It was painful to know he was only a few miles away, yet did not want to find out how she was, and it confirmed her belief that he wanted to be free of her.

In the morning, Juliet rang Lew Morgan to say she would accept the part in the historical serial, and within a week was busy with script meetings and costume fittings. She was out so much that she had her telephone switched through to an answering service, but the one call she longed for—though she did not openly admit it—never came, nor was there any communication from Damon's lawyer.

Luckily her work on the series was entertaining as well as hard, and for several hours each day she forgot her personal unhappiness. Yet she always thought of Damon last thing at night, and wondered if Monique was back in England. Because of his position in the medical world, she could not imagine him living with a woman openly, though he was sufficiently important to make his own rules in such a matter. It was amazing how little she knew of him—despite his brief association with her—and the knowledge that he might be sharing his home and bed with someone else filled her with jealousy that permeated her entire being.

The first daffodils were appearing in the florists' shops when Perry came to see her. One moment she was in the apartment alone and the next the doorbell rang and she opened it to see him standing in front of her, slim and vital as ever, his blue eyes twinkling and a faint smile animating his puckish features.

'Surprised to see me?' He stepped into the hall and presented her with a huge bunch of early spring flowers.

'How did you know where to find me?' Juliet asked.

'Lew told me. I didn't tell you I was coming because I wasn't sure if you'd see me.'

'Why shouldn't I? Actresses are always willing to see a famous film director.'

'You never loved me because of my fame,' he said, and put his arms around her.

Juliet kept the flowers in front of her and felt the stems crush as he ignored the bouquet and tightened his grip.

'Darling girl,' he murmured. 'If you'd refused to see me, I'd have understood why. I behaved like a swine.'

'You acted sensibly, Perry.' It was no effort for Juliet to keep her voice uncaring, since she no longer cared. 'It would have been kinder if you'd been less precipitate, but at least you were honest enough to admit you couldn't love someone who was less than perfect.'

'You positioned that knife perfectly, my angel,' he chuckled. 'And I'm going to show you how wrong you are. I should have taken you to Hollywood with me. You're worth a hundred Lilahs.' His eyes roamed her face. 'You're beautiful, Juliet. I've never seen you so radiant.'

Glad that looks could be deceptive, she gave him a wide smile and extricated herself from his hold. 'I hear you're directing a new film in England. Have you come to offer me a part?'

One eyebrow lifted in surprise; the Juliet of old would never have questioned him so bluntly.

'As a matter of fact I have. But let's not talk about it yet.'

'Why not?'

He laughed. 'My, my you've changed! You never used to be so aggressive.'

'I was, before I met you. I guess I've just reverted to type.'

'Can I revert you to the girl I knew?'

She heard the softness in his voice and recognised that he was marshalling his charm. But it no longer affected her and she drew a thankful breath. Thank heavens she was inoculated against the Perrys of this world. It had been a painful process, but worthwhile.

'I like myself the way I am,' she said calmly. 'And I intend to stay this way. One can't turn back the clock.'

'I'll believe that when you fall in love with some-one else. I must say I was amazed when I heard you'd married Masters, and even more astonished when I heard you left him.'

'Who told you?' she asked.

'Lew. Don't be annoyed with him, angel. You can't keep these things a secret. I'd already phoned Masters' house and found out you weren't there.'

Perry paced the room, restless as ever, Juliet was dis-turbed by his inability to relax, and knew she was comparing him unfavourably with Damon. If I don't stop doing that, she thought bitterly, I'll never make another life for myself.

'Tell me about the part,' she said aloud.

'It's a good one. I've brought a script along to show you. It isn't the lead—your name isn't big enough for that yet—but it's the best minor role, and I'll help you build it into a major one.'

'I'm not sure I have time to make a film,' she replied. 'I'm doing a TV series.'

'You can do both,' Perry said firmly. 'I've checked with Lew and he wants you to do it.'

'I'll read the script first. No one tells me what to do any more. I'm my own mistress now.'

'I should have made you mine when I had the chance,' Perry said ruefully.

Silently Juliet went to the door. 'I don't want to push you, Perry, but I've a date.' His nostrils thinned with irritation, but she pretended not to see it. 'I'll read the script and call you.'

'Good. I'm back to my old Juliet, so you see, things haven't changed as much as you think.'

'They have for me,' she replied, and silently thanked God for it.

That night she read the script and knew at once that Jacqueline could have been written for her. Next day she told Lew she would accept the part and left it to him to draw up the contract.

A week later the evening papers were ablaze with photographs of the stars who were taking part in the new Perry Langdon production, and her own picture was prominent among them.

As if to remind her that acting was only a game and that she should not allow herself to lose sight of reality, she collapsed twice the following day, and knew a dreadful fear that her illness was worsening—despite what Damon had told her. But nothing would induce her to call him, and instead she went to see Dr Clarendon.

'I've a note on my pad to call you tomorrow,' he greeted her. 'You must be psychic.'

'Only dreadfully worried. I think I'm getting worse.'

'On the contrary, you'll soon be getting better.'

He lifted a letter from his desk. It was on thick cream paper, typewritten but with a strong black signature at the bottom of the page. Her heart thumped and she was certain the letter was from Damon.

It was; and the news it contained was unbelievable. A new drug was being manufactured in America which would supply Juliet's body with the particular substance it needed to combat her illness.

'It was reported in *The Lancet* some while ago,' Dr Clarendon informed her, 'but I didn't let you know because the drug won't be on the market for six months. However, Dr Masters is a personal friend of Professor Laslo—the biochemist who discovered the drug—and he persuaded him to let him have a special supply, which he immediately sent on to me.' Dr Clarendon tapped a squat, round bottle that stood in front of him. 'All you need do is take one capsule last thing at night. Three months from now you should be completely cured.'

Juliet tried to speak but couldn't. Her throat was thick with tears and she swallowed hard.

'I can't believe ... I never imagined....' She leaned forward. 'How soon will the pills take effect?'

'By this time tomorrow you should be able to forget

you ever had any problems with your legs. But it takes between three and six months for the drug to make the effect permanent.' Dr Clarendon gave her a warm smile. 'It's wonderful for us when we can present a patient with a cure as simple as this. I only wish it happened more frequently.'

Buoyant with happiness, Juliet had to share it with someone. Diana was on tour with a play and Lew had flown to New York to watch the debut of one of his protegees. Only Perry was in London and she felt it inappropriate to share her joy with him, when he had left her alone to suffer her pain.

Reluctantly she went home—buying half a bottle of champagne on the way—and solemnly toasting herself in the mirror until she had finished it. Only then did she burst into tears, crying for happiness but also for Damon.

If he had wanted to get in touch with her again, the capsules had given him a wonderful opportunity. Instead he had written to Dr Clarendon, thus showing her quite clearly that their relationship was once more a purely medical one. Considering he had once said they were friends, it seemed an extraordinarily callous way to behave. After all, *he* had asked her to marry him, not the other way around; nor was she preventing him from obtaining his freedom. Bitterness engulfed her and her tears flowed faster. How futile her successful career seemed, compared with the life Monique was enjoying with Damon.

Resolutely she wiped her eyes and went into the bedroom to look at the bottle of capsules beside her bed. Health was more essential than love. She must remember that and be thankful.

CHAPTER FOURTEEN

JULIET meandered down Portland Place towards the BBC. She was due to attend a script conference there at three o'clock and had time to spare. She stopped and tilted her face to the pale sun. It looked like a slice of lemon in a water-washed blue sky, and there was a hint of rain in the air. It wasn't surprising, for April was only a couple of days away.

She lowered her head and continued to walk, forcibly resisting the urge to give a little skip and a jump as she did so. How wonderful to know her legs would not give way under her. The pills had done everything Dr Clarendon had promised and she could now lead a normal life, though the scars of fear would always remain with her.

Yet to the world at large she appeared totally serene: a beautifully dressed young woman with an aura of self-confidence that spoke of success. She was thinner than she had been in Doria—not from dieting but because she had too many private moments of anguish—and there were faint shadows beneath her sherry-brown eyes, though they were well hidden by make-up.

She reached the Weymouth Street intersection and stopped. The lights had changed and traffic streamed past her. A taxi pulled in to the kerb and a tall woman with auburn hair stepped out of it. There was something familiar about her, but it was not until she turned that Juliet recognised Monique.

Monique saw her at the same time and ran forward, hands outstretched.

'Juliet, how great to see you! I was thinking of you only the other day.'

Wryly Juliet wondered what the woman would say if she replied that *she* was constantly thinking of Monique and picturing her with Damon.

'You look marvellous,' Monique continued. 'You've lost your tan, though.'

'You haven't,' answered Juliet.

'I haven't had the chance. I bask in the sun like a lizard whenever I get the time.' Involuntarily Juliet glanced at the sky and Monique chuckled. 'Not the British sun, honey. I'm running the Clinic in Doria.'

'Still?' Juliet was disbelieving. 'I know Damon left you there when he returned to London, but I thought you'd come back ages ago.'

Monique shook her head. 'I only came back now because I'm on my way to Montreal. I'm going back to sell my house; then I'm returning to Doria.'

'You don't mean you're staying there permanently?'

'For the next three years at least. The Shiek is building me an operating theatre and intensive care unit that will be the most up-to-date in the world.'

Juliet could make no sense from what she was hearing. Did this mean that Damon was going to Doria too? She could not see him giving up his London practice and tried to imagine what relationship he and Monique would have if they were separated by so many miles. One could hardly go to Doria for a week-end or even on a once a month basis.

'Why are you so surprised?' Monique asked.

'I thought Damon ... that you and....' Juliet

paused, not sure how to continue.

'You thought Damon was going back to Kuwan to finish his contract?'

'Yes.' Eagerly Juliet clutched at this. 'I know he promised the Sheik he'd run the Clinic for a year.'

'It wasn't until two months ago that the Clinic started to function properly again, and even the Sheik didn't expect Damon to hang around until it did. By the time things were working normally, Damon had resumed his practice in London and wouldn't pull out again. Added to which,' Monique continued with a twinkle, 'I've made a little name for myself with the staff, and rather convinced His Oiliness that I wasn't such a bad replacement.'

'But what about you and Damon?' Juliet had not meant to ask the question, but nothing could stop it coming out.

Monique's look was wry. 'Are you asking if he loves me?'

'I took it for granted he did.'

'At the risk of sounding trite, I can only say that Damon sees me as a friend. He never saw me in any other way.'

A group of people walked past and one of them bumped against Juliet, who half-staggered.

Monique steadied her, then pulled back slightly, as if preparing herself for what she wanted to say.

'Damon's in love with *you*. We've never talked about it—you know what a clam he can be—but I'm willing to bet he was in love with you when he asked you to marry him.'

Juliet absorbed the words slowly, as if each one had to penetrate deep into her soul. 'You're wrong. He

asked me to marry him because he needed a wife. He
wouldn't have been able to do his work in Doria unless
he was married.'

'He never had any intention of working there. No
one would expect a man of Damon's stature to stick
himself in the middle of nowhere for twelve months—
no matter how magnificent the Clinic was. Sheik
Quima knew *that* right from the start.'

'Then why did Damon——'

'Go there? Because it gave him the excuse he needed
to marry you. He loved you, for God's sake. He still
does.'

Juliet shivered violently. 'He never said so.'

'He thinks you still want your ex-fiancé.' Monique
gave an exclamation of despair. 'What are you going to
do now?'

'Nothing.'

'But if you love him. . . .'

'I still think you've got it wrong. Maybe Damon isn't
in love with you—as I thought—but that still doesn't
mean he loves me. If he did, he'd have got in touch
with me when that new drug was discovered. I suppose you know about it?'

'Know about it?' Monique echoed. 'Damon spoke of
nothing else for weeks! He was on the phone to the
States every other day to find out how soon he could get
hold of it. If he didn't contact you about it himself,
it's because he didn't want to give you another reason
for being grateful to him.' Monique glanced at her
watch and pulled a face. 'I must fly. I'm already late
for an appointment. Think over what I've said, Juliet.
Damon wants you, but he'll never tell you. If you
love him, you'll have to make the first move.'

Before Juliet could reply, Monique was walking

away, her step confident, her auburn head high. A charming woman and a good one.

How small she makes me feel, Juliet thought, and knew that pride would never prevent Monique from fighting for her happiness. Yet it was unthinkable to go to Damon and confess she loved him. What if Monique was imagining it all? The way she herself had imagined so much that had turned out to be untrue.

For the rest of the afternoon she had to forget her own problems and think of the character she was portraying, and it was with enormous relief that she once more found herself in Portland Place, walking in the direction of Regents Park.

She knew what she wanted to do, but doubt held her back. Perhaps Damon had pretended he was in love with her in order to avoid involvement with Monique. In that way Monique's pride would not be hurt.

A taxi deposited a fare in front of her, and because it was the rush hour, she grabbed it and gave the driver her address. He did a U-turn and they headed west.

I'm a rotten coward, Juliet decided. Only an hour ago I was over the moon with delight at having my health restored, and now I don't have the guts to tell the man who helped me while I was ill that I love him. What does it matter if Monique is wrong and I find out he doesn't love me? At least I'll have done everything possible to bring us together.

Leaning forward, she gave the driver Damon's address in Harley Street. It was Thursday and, if he still kept to his previous routine, he would be seeing private patients.

The first time she had gone to see him had been a Thursday too. She remembered him saying he would have fitted her in earlier had he known she was Julia Stornaway, the actress. It was odd she should think of this today. He had also said he had seen her last play, and that he went to the theatre frequently. Yet in their many conversations since, he had never shown much knowledge of the theatre, and she wondered if he had feigned an interest merely to hide the fact that he had gone to see her on stage immediately after their very first meeting, when she had collapsed in front of his car. If that were so, then he had obviously been attracted to her from the beginning.

Hope began to rise. They were in Harley Street and she scanned the houses, her breath catching as they stopped outside the shiny black door with its well-polished brass knocker.

Quickly she ran up the steps and rang the bell, forcing herself to a calm she did not feel.

The door opened and Miss Benson stood there. She looked amazed but quickly controlled herself. She had seen Juliet many times during her stay in the house after her return from Doria, and must have wondered why she had left so suddenly.

'Is my—is Dr Masters in?' Juliet asked.

'He has a patient with him. But it's the last one.'

'Then I'll go into the waiting room.

Juliet was aware of the secretary's embarrassment, for the woman had not been sure whether to ask her to go upstairs to Damon's apartment. There were voices at the far end of the hall: Damon's deep one and the lighter tones of a woman.

'Dr Masters' patient is leaving,' Miss Benson said. 'I'll tell him you're here.'

'I'll tell him myself.'

As Miss Benson accompanied the patient to the door, Juliet went swiftly down the corridor to Damon's room. Without giving herself time to change her mind, she knocked on the door and entered. He was by the desk and had his back to her.

'There's no need for you to stay on, Miss Benson. I have some work to do, but I'll tape it. If you——' He turned, saw Juliet and was instantly silent.

Juliet stared at him. He was noticeably thinner and it made him look taller. The spattering of grey at his temples had become two distinctive wings of silver. They made him look more austere but very distinguished. How could a man like Damon love someone as lightweight as herself? Her courage ebbed fast, but she clung on to it.

'Hello, Damon,' she said huskily. 'I—er—I bumped into Monique this afternoon. She told me she's working in Doria. That's why I . . . why I came here.'

'I see.' Damon did not sound as if he did. He took a step forward, then stopped and motioned her to a chair. 'Come and sit down, Juliet. There's no need for you to stand by the door like a stranger.'

'It's how I feel.' She was shaking too much to move and she remained where she was. 'I thought you— that you were—were in love with Monique,' she said jerkily. 'I thought that's why you sent me away from Doria—because I stood between you and. . . .' Juliet's voice trailed away and she waited for Damon to say something; to say anything that would alleviate her embarrassment.

But he said nothing. He moved back against his desk and leaned on the side of it, arms folded across his chest.

'Haven't you anything to say?' she burst out.

His expression was unfathomable. 'You have a vivid imagination.'

'Sometimes too much, sometimes too little.'

'Too little?'

She took a deep breath. It was now or never. 'I—I didn't for one moment think you were in love with *me*.'

She waited for him to speak, but again he remained silent. This was much worse than she had anticipated, but it was too late for her to retract what she had said. She had to go on to the end, regardless of how bitter it turned out to be for her.

'Do you love me, Damon?' she asked flatly.

'Will you walk out if I say no?'

She flinched but stayed where she was. 'No. Whatever you feel for me makes no difference to the way *I* feel for you. I love you. I knew it when we were in Doria, but I didn't think you wanted me. I thought it was Monique.'

Two strides brought him to her side. A thin blue vein twitched at the corner of his eye and he put his hand to it. For an instant he looked intensely vulnerable and her heart seemed to turn over in her breast.

'You're everything I've ever wanted in a man,' she whispered. 'I was mad not to know it the first time I met you.'

'I knew how *I* felt from the beginning.'

Did this faint voice belong to Damon? Deeply moved, she put her hand on his arm. He seemed to gather strength from her touch, for when he spoke again, his voice was steadier.

'Maybe I should have told you how I felt, but you were ill and lonely and I didn't want to take advantage of you.'

'You invented a reason for marrying me,' she reminded him. 'Wasn't *that* taking advantage?'

'I did promise you your freedom after a year, if you wanted it. I thought you might go back to Langdon.'

'That silly man?'

Her choice of words, rather than their forcefulness, lightened Damon's expression, and he looked as if a weight had fallen from his shoulders. Gathering her into his arms, he held her so tightly that she could hardly breathe.

'Are you really here, Juliet, or will I wake up and find it's another dream?'

'Keep holding me and find out.'

She clung to him, running her hands over his face and hair before burying her head against the side of his neck. How clean and cool he smelled. Faintly astringent too, though there was nothing astringent in the passionate way his mouth was raining kisses upon her face.

'Why today?' he murmured huskily. 'Why today, when I'd finally decided I couldn't go on without you? Did you know I was coming to see you tonight?'

'Were you really?' She pulled back from him; not too far because she wanted him close, but enough for her to look into his eyes. 'Honestly, Damon?'

'Honestly, my darling. I wanted you so much that I was prepared to have you back on any terms, even a temporary one. But what about you? Are you really here because of Monique?'

'Yes. Until this afternoon I thought you were with her.'

'Professionally only.' Humour edged his voice and he ran a finger down the side of her cheek. 'You're young and beautiful and you have an exciting career in front of you. Why should you want to tie yourself to a man who spends half his time in hospital and the other half in his consulting-room?'

'Because I'm a masochist!' she said. 'Besides, you have to eat and sleep some time.'

'I'll forgo the eating,' he whispered, finding her mouth with his own.

As he felt her softness, his body hardened. It was beyond his control to stop it, and Juliet knew a thrill of triumph at the realisation of the power she had over him. She would use it to protect him; to give him the peace he deserved.

'And the pleasure too,' she murmured. 'Oh, my darling, how I'll pleasure you!'

'Now,' he said thickly, rubbing his lips against hers. 'I want you so much.'

'And I want you. For the rest of my life, Damon. I thought that having a career would help me to forget how much I loved you, but it only made it worse.'

'I know how you feel.' His hands moved across her waist and then rose to cup her breasts. 'Let's get out of this room before I do something I've never done here before.'

The gleam in his eyes told what he meant and she moved with him to the door. Miss Benson had tactfully left for the day and the hall was empty as they entered the small lift and pressed the button.

Quietly it carried them to the top floor and heaven.

The Mills & Boon Rose is the Rose of Romance

Every month there are ten new titles to choose from — ten new stories about people falling in love, people you want to read about, people in exciting, far-away places. Choose Mills & Boon. It's your way of relaxing:

October's titles are:

NO PASSING FANCY by Kay Thorpe
Claire's father had tricked her into going out to Tanzania, and there she found herself thrown into the company of the forceful Rod Gilvray.

HEART OF STONE by Janet Dailey
'I live hard and fast and love the same way,' declared Brock Canfield. At least Stephanie knew where she stood — but was what he offered enough for her?

WIFE BY CONTRACT by Flora Kidd
Her marriage to Damien Nikerios had brought Teri money and position — and the humiliation of knowing that Damien had only married her as a cover-up for his affair with his father's wife.

WHEN LIGHTNING STRIKES by Jane Donnelly
Robina had an abiding detestation of Leo Morgan who was responsible for so much of her unhappiness. And yet her life seemed to be inextricably involved with him . . .

SHADOW OF DESIRE by Sara Craven
Ginny needed to keep Max Henrick at more than arm's length — which wasn't going to be easy when she was living and working in the same house.

FEAR OF LOVE by Carole Mortimer
If Alexandra wanted to marry Roger Young, that, she felt, was her own affair. Just what business was it of the high-handed Dominic Tempest?

WIFE FOR A YEAR by Roberta Leigh
Juliet had married Damon Masters to enable him to take an important job in one of the Gulf states. She had no feeling for him — or so she thought . . .

THE WINDS OF WINTER by Sandra Field
Anne Metcalfe had assumed a new name and identity to return, after four years, to her husband's house. She just *had* to discover if what she suspected was true . . .

FLAMINGO PARK by Margaret Way
What right did Nick Langford have to try and run Kendall's life for her? She was quite capable of looking after herself — wasn't she?

SWEET NOT ALWAYS by Karen van der Zee
Was Jacqueline's job in Ghana the real challenge, or was it Matt Simmons, her boss, who seemed so determined to think badly of her?

Mills & Boon Classics

The very best of Mills & Boon
romances, brought back for those of you
who missed reading them when they
were first published.

In
October
we bring back the following four
great romantic titles.

NO QUARTER ASKED
by Janet Dailey
Stacy Adams was a rich girl who wanted to sample real life for
a change, so she courageously took herself off alone to Texas
for a while. It was obvious from the first that the arrogant
rancher Cord Harris, for some reason, disapproved of her — but
why should she care what he thought?

MIRANDA'S MARRIAGE
by Margery Hilton
Desperation forced Miranda to encamp for the night in Jason
Steele's office suite, but unfortunately he found her there, and
after the unholy wrath that resulted she never dreamed that a
few months later she would become his wife. For Jason was
reputed to be a rake where women were concerned. So what
chance of happiness had Miranda?

THE LIBRARY TREE
by Lilian Peake
Carolyn Lyle was the niece of a very influential man, and
nothing would convince her new boss, that iceberg Richard
Hindon, that she was nothing but a spoiled, pampered darling
who couldn't be got rid of fast enough! Had she even got time
to make him change his mind about her?

PALACE OF THE POMEGRANATE
by Violet Winspear
Life had not been an easy ride for Grace Wilde and she had
every reason to be distrustful of men. Then, in the Persian
desert, she fell into the hands of another man. Kharim Khan,
who was different from any other man she had met . . .

Give yourself and your friends a romantic Christmas.

First time in paperback, four superb romances by favourite authors, in an attractive maroon and gold gift pack. A superb present to give. And to receive.

Sandstorm
Anne Mather

Lord of the High Valley
Margaret Way

Man's World
Charlotte Lamb

Enemy In Camp
Janet Dailey

United Kingdom	£2.60
Rep. of Ireland	£2.86
Publication	10th October 1980

Look for this gift pack at your local Mills & Boon stockist.

Doctor Nurse Romances

and October's
stories of romantic relationships behind the scenes
of modern medical life are:

SURGEON'S CHALLENGE
by Helen Upshall

Sister Claire Tyndall's success as a nurse was undoubted
— but as a woman? Richard Lynch and Dr Alan Jarvis
both made it clear that they were interested in her. Both
were handsome and determined, but both — unfortunately
for Claire — seemed to be married already!

ATTACHED TO DOCTOR MARCHMONT
by Juliet Shore

Doctor Sally Preston's relationship with her new chief,
Darien Marchmont, got off to a sticky start. So she was
less than pleased to discover that their first joint
assignment was a two-man medical survey in the heart
of the North African desert!

ORDER NOW FOR DIRECT DELIVERY

Choose from this selection of

Mills & Boon 🌳 FAVOURITES

—ALL HIGHLY RECOMMENDED

☐ C259
SONG IN MY HEART
Rachel Lindsay

☐ C260
THE GLASS CASTLE
Violet Winspear

☐ C261
INTERLUDE IN ARCADY
Margery Hilton

☐ C262
THE INNOCENT INVADER
Anne Mather

☐ C263
SILVER FRUIT UPON
SILVER TREES
Anne Mather

☐ C264
THE REAL THING
Lilian Peake

☐ C265
BLACK NIALL
Mary Wibberley

☐ C266
COUSIN MARK
Elizabeth Ashton

☐ C267
NO FRIEND OF MINE
Lilian Peake

☑ C268
THE ARROGANCE OF
LOVE
Anne Mather

☐ C269
THE BRIDE OF ROMANO
Rebecca Stratton

☐ C270
SHADE OF THE PALMS
Roberta Leigh

ONLY **65p** EACH

SIMPLY TICK ☑ YOUR SELECTION(S)
ABOVE, THEN JUST COMPLETE AND
POST THE ORDER FORM OVERLEAF ▸